Off
the Map

ALSO BY TRISH DOLLER

Adult Novels

Float Plan

The Suite Spot

Young Adult Novels

Something Like Normal

Where the Stars Still Shine

The Devil You Know

In a Perfect World

Start Here

Off the Map

TRISH DOLLER

ST. MARTIN'S
GRIFFIN
NEW YORK

First published in the United States by St. Martin's Griffin, an imprint of St. Martin's Publishing Group

OFF THE MAP. Copyright © 2023 by Trish Doller. All rights reserved. Printed in the United States of America. For information, address St. Martin's Publishing Group, 120 Broadway, New York, NY 10271.

www.stmartins.com

Designed by Omar Chapa

Library of Congress Cataloging-in-Publication Data

Names: Doller, Trish, author.
Title: Off the map : a novel / Trish Doller.
Description: First edition. | New York : St. Martin's Griffin, 2023.
Identifiers: LCCN 2022048295 | ISBN 9781250809490 (trade paperback) | ISBN 9781250809506 (ebook)
Classification: LCC PS3604.O4357 O44 2023 | DDC 813/.6—dc23
LC record available at https://lccn.loc.gov/2022048295

Our books may be purchased in bulk for promotional, educational, or business use. Please contact your local bookseller or the Macmillan Corporate and Premium Sales Department at 1-800-221-7945, extension 5442, or by email at MacmillanSpecialMarkets@macmillan.com.

First Edition: 2023

10 9 8 7 6 5 4 3 2 1

To the real Carla Black

I have found out that there ain't no surer way to find out whether you like people or hate them than to travel with them.

—MARK TWAIN

Chapter 1

My dad always says that the people waiting for you at the airport should never be strangers. They should be family members, overjoyed to reunite after being separated—even if it's only been a few days. Or lovers, so impatient to see you that they sweep you into their arms and kiss you passionately in public. Or maybe even close friends, excited to create new memories and reminisce about the old.

Dad doesn't believe in searching for cardboard signs with your name printed in black Sharpie letters or awkwardly scanning faces, wondering if that brown-haired man—the one standing beside the ugly modern art sculpture that all airports seem to have—is the person you're seeking. And according to Biggie Black, if meeting a stranger at the airport is unavoidable, there is nowhere less inspiring than the Air Margaritaville.

So, when my plane touches down at Dublin Airport, and I switch on my phone for the first time since my layover in Philly, I'm pleased to find a text from Eamon Sullivan, asking me to meet him in a pub near the city center. Bars don't necessarily make identifying strangers any easier, but it's a much more interesting origin story if you eventually become friends. And if you happen to ID the wrong guy in the bar, you can always blame it on the booze.

The name of the pub is The Confession Box, which calls to mind scandalous secrets, clandestine affairs, and alcohol flowing freely enough to loosen tongues. It sounds like it might be a seedy little dive in the wrong part of town. It sounds like my kind of place. I smile to myself, wondering what this choice says about Eamon Sullivan.

I respond: PERFECT. JUST LANDED.

My fellow passengers begin to rouse like zombies as our plane taxis toward the terminal. Biggie taught me to wait in my seat until the plane has formally arrived, out of respect for the flight crew, but also because there's no point in launching yourself into the aisle when there's nowhere to go. All around me, electronics are stowed. Neck pillows removed. Personal belongings moved from beneath the seat in front of them to their laps, their legs bouncing, waiting to spring up. The wheels have barely stopped moving before the overhead bins are thrown open and the aisle is clogged with people waiting to get off the plane.

Another nugget of wisdom from my dad: *Why hurry up and wait when you can simply wait?*

For a man who holds no specific religious beliefs, Biggie's attitude is remarkably Zen. But after visits to thirteen countries and the lower forty-eight states, I have never known his advice to fail me. I stretch out my legs in the emergency exit row with Social Distortion pulsing through my headphones as the horde shambles past. Once the other passengers are through the jet bridge, I sling my backpack over my shoulder and disembark, thanking the crew as I go. By the time I reach the immigration queue, most of the people from my flight are now behind me in line, having rushed off the plane for a reviving cup of coffee, to use the bathroom, or to claim their luggage.

● ● ●

My passport stamped and nothing of value to declare, I pause to pull a bit of cash from a nearby ATM before exiting the airport. I follow the signs down the escalator to the taxi stand, where I hail a cab and direct the driver to take me to The Confession Box.

Dublin rolls past my window—low-rise buildings in shades of brown and gray—and I think about how often people ask me if I'm afraid to travel by myself. They wonder if it's lonely to eat in restaurants or drink in bars alone. They fear I might be robbed or kidnapped or worse. But eight years ago, Biggie Black—traveling partner, best friend, father—was diagnosed with early onset dementia. In the days following his diagnosis, he decided he didn't want me to see him deteriorate. He forbade me from waiting around for him to forget me.

"You only get so many trips around the sun," he said, tapping his first two fingers against his temple. "And some of us don't even get to keep the memories until our lights go out."

He dug his hand into the front pocket of his old baggy jeans and pulled out a set of keys. They were looped on a key chain that was a bottle opener from a craft brewery in Nashville, and I recognized them at once—the keys to his chili-pepper-red Jeep Wrangler.

Biggie had bought the Jeep brand new when I was a little girl, not long after my mom left. Eventually, he'd removed the back seat and built a wooden platform in the cargo area to create additional space for camping equipment. That summer, and every summer after, he'd taken me off-roading and overlanding across the United States, teaching me geography, history, and engine repair along the way. I loved that Jeep almost as much as I loved him. But as he folded the keys into my palm, tears welled up in my eyes and I shook my head. "Biggie, no. I can't—"

"Listen, I've still got some time before the holes in my memory start getting bigger," he said, cutting me off. "But Valentina was always gonna be yours one day. Today might as well be the day."

I tried to imagine what it would be like to travel without him, but it was like looking into a lake so deep you couldn't see the bottom. Unfathomable. "What are you going to do?"

"Oh, I think it's time for me and Stella to get hitched," he said, referring to his longtime girlfriend, whom he'd never once mentioned asking to be his wife.

I fell against him, sobbing into his shoulder. "I don't want to lose you, Biggie."

"You aren't losing me," he said, his big, thick arms wrapping around me, holding me tight. "I taught you everything you know, so I will *always* be with you."

He pulled back a little and tilted my chin. I may have inherited the height gene, but I still had to look up at him. He swam in my vision. "What's the family motto?"

Biggie had invented the family motto when I was going through my thirteen-year-old asshole phase, questioning why we had to spend yet another summer climbing over boulders and sleeping on the ground. It had been the one year in my life I wanted to do ordinary teenage things, like sleeping in on the weekend, hanging out on the beach with friends, and maybe kissing boys. But Dad had long ago decided that our lives should be extraordinary.

My laugh was thick with snot and tears, and I wiped my eyes with the heels of my hands. "Here for a good time, not for a long time."

Biggie shrugged and did that thing with his mouth that

he imagined made him look like De Niro, but since he looked nothing like De Niro, it only made him look slightly constipated. "Exactly. It's going to be okay. I've got no regrets, and I don't want you to have any either. Look forward, Carla, not back."

Now, when people ask me if I'm afraid to travel alone, I always tell them no. After all, what could possibly happen to me that's worse than having my dad disappear, piece by tiny piece?

• • •

The Confession Box turns out to be a traditional Irish pub, but not the touristy red one with the riotous flower boxes that shows up in a lot of travel photos of Dublin. Not that there's anything wrong with tourist attractions. They have their place. No, the exterior of The Confession Box is painted glossy black and trimmed with gold leaf paint that shines in the sun. Guinness signs hang in the front window, and a black sandwich board on the pavement claims the pub was once the favorite of Irish revolutionary Michael Collins.

I snap a quick selfie and text it to Stella so she can show Biggie. Maybe he'll recognize me today, maybe he won't. His memory is growing more unpredictable, and every text, every call, every video chat is a crapshoot.

I step inside the pub and realize almost at once that there's little chance of missing Eamon Sullivan. There are only about ten seats at the bar, a handful of small tables around the perimeter, and a little upper balcony. It's not a seedy dive, it's simply *tiny*. The name makes sense in a whole different context and I'm not disappointed.

Dropping my backpack on the floor below the bar, I hoist myself onto a wooden barstool. A bank of taps to my left offers a variety of beers and ciders, but I'm in Ireland, so I order a pint of Guinness.

Every bartender worth their salt knows that a proper Guinness pour is both a science and an art. The glass needs to be held at the proper angle, and you only fill the glass three-quarters of the way before letting it rest for almost two minutes. Or 119.53 seconds, to be precise. Back home in Fort Lauderdale, I work as a bartender in a pirate-themed bar where the waitress uniforms look like the result you'd get if you googled "sexy pirate costume." My own uniform is a black tank top that says WENCH across the back. Since our customers are bedazzled by boobs and legs, a proper Guinness pour is usually the last thing they care about.

As I settle in to wait for my beer and Eamon's arrival, I text Anna to let her know I've arrived in Ireland.

ARE YOU ON YOUR WAY TO TRALEE? she responds.

NOT YET, BUT EAMON SHOULD BE HERE SOON, I tap out.

Anna has been my best friend since our very first shift together at the bar. Maybe it's because we'd both grown up in single-parent homes. Or because neither of us knew how it felt to be born with silver spoons in our mouths. Or because working in a tits-and-ass restaurant was a deliberate career choice and not a layover on our way to a "real" job. Most people don't get closer than arm's length with me, so maybe the real reason we're friends is that neither of us expects more than the other is able to give.

Every spring, when snowbird season ends in South Florida, I pack my shit into Valentina—nicknamed after my dad's favorite Mexican hot sauce—and head in whichever direction my internal compass points. I've always known that Anna would be there when I returned. After her fiancé Ben died, she took off sailing, and I understood why she had to leave.

Although she hasn't officially returned to Florida, the last time I saw Anna, her spirit was restored, and her heart was in the hands of someone new. Someone worthy. So, when she asked me to fly to Ireland and stand beside her when she marries Keane Sullivan, the only possible answer was yes.

The barman rests a pint of Guinness on a beer mat in front of me.

"Thank you." I stash my phone in the back pocket of my jeans and glance around the room for anyone who might resemble Eamon. Anna told me he was a few inches shorter, slightly older, and significantly less scruffy than Keane, which means Eamon will probably have dark brown hair, possibly hazel eyes, and a killer smile. No one in the pub fits that description, so I take a long swallow of beer and sigh with satisfaction. "From one bartender to another, this might be the best Guinness I've ever had."

The barman gives a knowing chuckle as he nods. "You wouldn't be the first to say it."

The deeper I dive into my glass, the more the travel fatigue falls away. The minute hand of the clock above the bar ticks steadily past noon and The Confession Box starts drawing a crowd—well, a tiny crowd. I order a second pint as a guy wearing business casual gray pants and a white button-up shirt claims the barstool to my right. I sneak a glance from the corner of my eye, but he has ginger hair and freckles, neither of which Anna mentioned.

Not Eamon.

The guy orders a pint of Magners cider and swivels toward me. "American?"

I don't really feel much like being chatted up by a stranger, but one of the first rules of bar etiquette is that you don't ignore the people sitting beside you. If you want privacy, you choose a table. That doesn't mean you have to endure hours—or even minutes—of unwanted conversation, but you should at least be polite.

"Yes."

"Welcome to Dublin." He touches his chest. "The name's Gavin."

"Carla."

"Lovely to meet you." His voice is slightly raspy, and his Irish accent is sexy, which bumps his attractiveness level up another notch. Not enough for me to want to change my plans and be *interested,* but enough to pass the time until Eamon arrives. "What part of America are you from?"

I give a short, sharp laugh. "The worst part."

"Ah," Gavin says, knowingly. "You must be from Florida."

I point a finger at him. "Got it in one."

He laughs and loosens the next button on his shirt. "What do you do there?"

"I'm a bartender. How 'bout you?"

"Tech." Gavin takes a huge swig of cider and wipes the dribble from his chin with the back of his hand. His stock drops a few points, but I've seen worse from the other side of the bar. "Dublin is a center for IT."

I'm not anti-technology. I text, email, and post my adventures on social media as much as the next person. In fact, my Instagram account has a ridiculous number of followers because I'm an attractive woman doing "dude" things in a Jeep. But the idea of sitting behind a computer all day doing . . . *anything* . . . sounds like a soul-sucking hell. I'd probably be drinking Magners at noon on a Monday, too.

"What brings you to Ireland?" Gavin asks.

"My best friend is getting married this weekend."

He winks but puts too much cheek in it to be charming. "Need a plus-one?"

Before I have a chance to answer, the front door opens and a man walks into the bar who not only fits Anna's description of Eamon, but exceeds her description, and grinds her description into fine sand. It's like trying to stare directly at an eclipse and not go blind.

Gavin's question hangs in the air.

Eamon Sullivan stands only a few feet away, scanning the room.

He looks directly at me without a flicker of recognition.

Before my brain has time to consider the consequences, I shoot him my most brilliant smile, catch the front of his olive-green button-up shirt in my fist, and pull him toward me. "Oh my God, babe, you're finally here!"

His dark brows flex with momentary confusion, but when my lips brush against his, Eamon leans in to the improvisation. His fingertips land, warm and soft, against my neck. He angles his head, deepening the kiss. His thumb caresses my cheek, sending goose bumps racing across the backs of my arms. Eamon's mouth lingers on my lower lip as he slowly breaks away, leaving me dazed and breathless. He gives me the barest hint of a grin before grazing his lips against the middle of my forehead. "Jaysus, but I've missed you."

We stare at each other until Gavin's voice penetrates the bubble. "Well, then, never mind. I reckon you've managed to find a plus-one all on your own."

I laugh, bumping back to reality. "I do appreciate the offer."

As Gavin vacates his stool, he quickly assesses Eamon, casts a dubious eye at me, and snorts a laugh. "Sure you do."

"Not entirely certain what just happened," Eamon says, claiming the empty seat and indicating to the barman to set up another round. "But . . . hi, I'm Eamon. And you are?"

"I'm Carla."

"Carla." He blinks and realization dawns in his eyes. Green eyes, not hazel at all. "Oh. You're—*you*. I expected more luggage, less . . . kissing. Also, Anna said you'd have your hair done up in a messy bun and that you've got a full sleeve of tattoos, so you're not what I expected."

I ease back the cuff of my long-sleeved T-shirt, and Eamon's eyes fall on the collection of tiny stars that circle my wrist. My entire right arm is covered with black minimalist tattoos I've collected like souvenirs from the places I've traveled. Most of them are Sagittarius-related because if I have any faith at all, I have faith in the stars. Among them is a centaur on the back of my upper arm, inked at a shop in Barra de la Cruz, a bow made of flowers from a shop in Taos, and a stick-and-poke Sagittarius constellation that Biggie's friend Ugly Louie did in his garage in Dania Beach when I turned eighteen.

"Anna couldn't have known about the cooler weather," Eamon says, at the same time as I say, "She had no idea I was getting a haircut."

I touch the fringe at the back of my neck, still not used to the length. The stylist made me confirm several times that I really wanted a pixie cut. I've worn my hair in a bun for nearly a decade, hoping it might help Dad recognize me longer. But two weeks ago, during a video chat, he confused me for my mother and called me Sheryl. I realized the style of my hair doesn't matter anymore.

"For what it's worth, I think your hair looks lovely," Eamon says.

The warmth of his compliment floods my cheeks and I smile at him. "Thank you. I'm sorry about that weird"—I wave my hand in his general direction—"violation of your face. I don't normally kiss people without their permission."

His laugh makes it clear he's unfazed. "I take it that bloke was annoying you."

I hesitate. Gavin hadn't been particularly bothersome. He didn't have time to be persistent or make me feel uncomfortable. He wasn't acting sketchy or threatening. And I've never been especially shy about telling someone I'm not interested. But how can I possibly explain to Eamon—without sounding completely unhinged—that the impulse to kiss him struck me like a Holy Roller speaking in tongues? He does resemble his brother, but Keane's attractiveness is magnified by a giant helping of charisma, a dash of swagger, and perpetual sex hair, while Eamon's attractiveness needs no help at all. Both Sullivan brothers won the same genetic lottery, but Eamon is like when the Powerball jackpot hits a billion.

"He was." I throw in a nod with my big fat falsehood.

Eamon shrugs a single shoulder, and even the slightest hint of a smile makes his cheek dimple. "You'll get no complaints from me."

"You caught on quick."

"I happen to be a natural actor," he says. "At the primary school they still weep over my portrayal of Saint Joseph in the Nativity play."

"With joy or laughter?"

He cocks his head, considering, before the dimple deepens. "Bit of both, I reckon."

The barman has barely finished putting the next round of Guinness on the bar when Eamon grabs one of the glasses and takes a giant gulp. As his tongue slides out to lick away the pale foam clinging to his upper lip, my breath catches in my chest, and the thoughts I push out of my head are positively obscene.

Chapter 2

"Now my curiosity is piqued." I slide my empty glass aside to make room for the next round of Guinness. "What really happened during the Nativity play?"

Eamon rests his arm along the back of my chair, bringing his body closer to mine, as if we're old friends instead of brand-new acquaintances. A tiny cynical voice inside me wonders if this is one of his signature moves, but the warmth rolling through me doesn't care. I angle toward him to listen.

"The thing to keep in mind is that at the time I was a wee lad of five," he says. "But while the children's choir was singing 'Away in a Manger,' the baby Jesus—played by Taddy Finnegan, an actual baby—started squirming and scrunching up his face."

He pauses for a quick drink.

"A moment later, the most wretched odor began creeping

out of the manger," Eamon continues. "Having a younger brother, I was well versed in that smell, so I shouted, 'The baby Jesus has done a poo!'"

I let out a laugh. "Oh no."

He nods. "Oh yes. And to make matters worse, my older brother, Patrick, called back from the audience, 'You're his da. Clean it up.' Taking his advice literally, I lifted the baby, but his nappy was so loaded that it fell straight off, splattering poo all over the floor. Mrs. Finnegan rushed up onstage to rescue wee Taddy, but by then the crowd was roaring and the choir performance had fallen apart. I was banned from participating in the Nativity play, and to this day I'm not certain I'm allowed back in the building."

By the time he's finished, tears are trickling from the corners of my eyes and my sides hurt from laughing. "Between this story and some of the ones Keane has shared, your family sounds really fun."

"I haven't always seen it that way," Eamon says, his expression slipping into thoughtfulness. "But they're grand. What's your family like?"

"No siblings," I say. "But my dad is the best person I know, and he raised me by himself for most of my childhood." Before Eamon can ask about my mom, I forge on. "He was a high school history teacher, so we spent every summer traveling. He bought me a National Parks Passport and we set out to visit every park site in the contiguous United States."

"Did you?"

"It took nearly twenty years, but we visited three hundred and ninety-two of them."

"I don't believe you," he says, except his dimple appears. Teasing me.

I lean down and scoop my backpack off the floor. It's made of whiskey-brown leather—a gift from Biggie when I turned nine, along with the National Parks Passport and his first bit of traveler's wisdom: *If it doesn't fit in your backpack, you don't need it.*

The Parks Passport has had a permanent home in the front pocket ever since. I unbuckle the pocket and hand over the small, worn, spiral-bound book. Some of the pages are falling out, so it's held together with a thick red rubber band.

Eamon pages carefully through the book, lingering to look at the cancellations—dated ink stamps pressed onto the pages by rangers from the various parks and monuments—and the panoramic stickers designed to look like postage stamps. After so many years, the Passport has become an unofficial diary. My face flushes at the unexpected intimacy of it. This is a glimpse behind a curtain most people aren't allowed to see, but for reasons I can't name, Eamon Sullivan seems like someone I can trust with the doodles, chocolate smears, notes, dried tears, and bits of my heart left among the pages.

"This is amazing," he says, a note of wonder in his voice, and I'm relieved that he doesn't poke fun at something so important to me. Relieved that my trust has not been misplaced. "I had no idea there were so many national parks in America."

"There are sixty-three major parks," I explain. "Those are the famous ones like Yellowstone. Yosemite. Grand Canyon. But . . . the rest . . . yeah. So many."

Eamon smiles and it makes me want to kiss him again. "Do you have a favorite?"

"The first time my dad and I traveled outside Florida, I was five," I say. "He took me to De Soto National Forest in Mississippi. It was an eleven-hour drive, but when we got there, we found a beautiful, secluded campsite beside a creek."

I turn the pages of the Passport until I find the one with map coordinates written in the margin.

"De Soto is not in this book," I tell Eamon. "Not sure why national forests don't count as national parks, but they don't, so Biggie—my dad—wrote the coordinates for our campsite, so I'd be able to find it again someday."

"Were you?"

Somewhere in my Instagram feed there's a photo taken during my return to De Soto—twenty years later—of me sitting on the hood of the Jeep with the muddy brown creek in the background. I consider showing him, but maybe he's more polite than interested.

"My dad made pizza in a cast-iron skillet over an open fire, and I was sure I'd never tasted anything so good," I continue.

"The next day, we found a spot where the creek widened into a swimming hole. A rope swing had been hung from a branch extending over the water, so we spent the whole afternoon dropping like cannonballs off the rope into the water."

There's a light in Eamon's eyes as he listens. Like he's not just being polite. And the desire to kiss him swells further in my chest. "What a special memory. Is that why De Soto is your favorite?"

"Mostly," I say, omitting the part about how my mother had walked out a few months earlier, leaving nothing but a note. How Dad bought the Jeep, outfitted it for camping, and took me on a summerlong adventure because he didn't know what else to do with a little girl who missed her mama. That first year he distracted me with rivers, mountains, and endless bags of marshmallows for toasting. I feel a small pang at the memory. "But . . . I have another favorite that's in the book."

"Hmm." Eamon scratches along his jawline like he's considering, before nodding. "Fine. I'll allow two favorites."

"Have you heard of Joshua Tree?"

"*I can't liiiiiive,*" he belts out, clutching the front of his shirt while flinging the other arm theatrically wide, nearly smacking the man sitting beside him, "*with or without you.*"

A few people at the bar chuckle at Eamon's off-key singing, and when I connect the dots, I laugh along with them. "Not *that Joshua Tree.*"

"I know." He winks, and it's a *great* wink. Keane may not

be the only Sullivan with a dash of swagger, but Eamon looks so pulled together that it's more surprising coming from him.

"I went backcountry camping at Joshua Tree a couple of years ago to watch the Leonid meteor shower," I tell him. "It was so dark that I couldn't see anything but stars. It felt like the sky was everywhere."

Eamon doesn't respond and his expression goes kind of . . . wistful . . . and I wonder where he's gone inside his head. I'm about to ask when I notice that the natural light streaming in from the windows of the upper balcony has dimmed. The clock above the bar shows that *hours* have passed while we've been talking. I dig my phone from my pocket to find one missed call and two text messages from Anna, wondering where we are. Double-checking that Eamon and I are not dead somewhere along the M7.

GOT A LITTLE SIDETRACKED AT THE PUB, I text back.

She responds with a crying laugh emoji, which I appreciate. Even though the wedding isn't until Saturday, she could be losing her shit instead of smiling. BE SAFE. SEE YOU WHEN I SEE YOU.

"Do you realize we should be on the other side of the country by now?" I ask Eamon, as I put my phone away.

"Oh, feck." His head jerks up and swivels, registering that the crowd around us has changed and there's a singer tuning an acoustic guitar in the corner near the fireplace. "I'm sorry. I completely lost track of time."

I'm reminded of another Biggie-ism. He always says you can never be truly lost. *If you just keep going in the same direction,* he'll say, *eventually you'll end up somewhere. It might not be where you intended to go, but you won't be lost anymore.*

His theory makes sense . . . in theory. But not every unplanned destination is a good one. One night, I ended up in a part of San Francisco where I hadn't meant to be. While I was stopped for gas, a man pulled a knife on me and demanded my wallet. The real one, with my credit cards and most of my cash, was locked in a security box Biggie had bolted to the floor beneath the driver's seat. Instead, I reached for a different wallet and opened it to reveal a twenty-dollar bill and a debit card.

"This is all I have," I said, before lobbing it over his shoulder.

He ran for the wallet, and I jumped into the Jeep, driving off without getting gas. The balance on the card was only about fifty bucks, a small price to pay for not being murdered.

I cock my head and smile at Eamon. "I guess we'll get there when we get there."

His eyes meet mine as he hands back my book. The wistfulness is gone, replaced by something that looks like yearning. But then he blinks, and it's gone. "Are you hungry at all?"

"Starving."

"You should have said something." He takes his wallet from the back pocket of his jeans and hands a credit card to the barman.

"Yeah, well . . . time got away from me, too."

Our eyes lock again, and this time I feel a seismic shift, a mutual acknowledgment that the afternoon wasn't lost at all. That maybe we've been right where we were meant to be. Maybe we still are.

There's almost always a singular moment when I know I'm going to sleep with someone. This is it. And the almost imperceptible lift at the corner of his mouth makes me think we've reached the same conclusion.

His eyes break away from mine only long enough for him to scribble his name at the bottom of the receipt. "There's a kebab shop on the way to my flat."

"Sounds perfect."

He hoists my backpack onto his shoulder and extends a hand. "Come on, then."

Outside, the air has cooled, but Eamon's hand around mine is warm, and the kebab restaurant is quite literally around the corner from the pub. The fragrant scent of roasting meat greets us as we enter the narrow shop.

I lean against the wall, studying Eamon as he orders döner kebabs and cans of Coke from the takeaway counter. His short, dark hair is parted on the side and combed neatly away from his face. His jeans fall into the perfect gap between loose-fitting and skinny, and the olive green of his shirt makes his eyes pop. He's learned how to play to his strengths, or someone is buying his clothes for him. Either way, I'm so distracted that we're halfway down the block when I realize I didn't even offer to pay.

He waves me off, stopping in front of an apartment building. "This is me."

Eamon unlocks a glass door that opens into a hallway with a bank of mailboxes on one side and a flight of stairs climbing the other. I follow him to an elevator near the back of the building. He presses the button for the fifth floor and the doors slide closed.

The air in the elevator nearly crackles with the tension growing between us, and as we stand side by side, watching the numbers ascend, Eamon says, "Just so you know, I'm going to kiss you again, but this time I'm going to mean it."

Heat spirals through me, settling heavy between my thighs. I don't look at him for fear I might combust. It's such a cliché—the maid of honor and the best man hooking up—but that's no reason to stop it from happening. "Okay, but we're not having sex until after I eat my kebab."

His laugh is low and slightly wicked. "That's fair."

The elevator chimes and the doors slide open. Eamon takes my hand again and leads me down the hall to his apartment. Inside, he dumps the takeaway bag and his keys on a small table beside the door and takes my face in his hands. His mouth covers mine, and when his tongue teases along the seam of my lips, I let him in, hungry in a different kind of way. His hands shift to my hips, and when I slip my arms around his neck, he pulls me closer. I want him so badly, but I'm not ready for this to escalate yet. I need food and to wash away 4,000 miles' worth of travel funk before I let Eamon see me naked. But when his palm curves around my ass and I feel his body, ready for mine, my excuses turn to white noise. I sink my hands into his hair, the strands thick and soft as they run through my fingers. Eamon groans into my mouth.

"Jaysus." He's panting as he releases me. "I thought I was playing it cool back there in the lift, but you've completely unraveled me. We, uh—" He clears his throat. "We'd better eat those kebabs before I make a mess of myself."

"And I haven't had a shower since yesterday, so . . ."

"I wasn't going to mention it," Eamon says, grabbing the takeaway bag. His apartment is an open floor plan, so it's only a few steps from the door to the kitchen. "But you do smell a bit like Taddy Finnegan's arse."

I punch his shoulder, and he laughs, leaning down to kiss me. Again, he forces himself away, like I'm some kind of sexy tractor beam. "When you're done with your kebab, I'll show you to the bath."

We eat at a small mid-century-style table beside a non-working fireplace filled with plants. The apartment isn't huge, but the ceilings soar, and the windows are tall. The walls are painted crisp white, and Eamon's furniture is pale beige, scattered with neutral throw pillows. Two large geometric art prints hang on the wall. The whole apartment has a minimalist

Scandinavian-but-not-IKEA vibe. Like something that would be featured on the Apartment Therapy website for its perfection. Except it feels like a place people live *around,* rather than *in.* There's not even a dent on the couch bearing evidence that someone sits on it. I've only known Eamon about a minute, but this doesn't feel like *him.*

"Did you decorate this apartment yourself?" I ask, shredding the kebab paper into tiny bits. Having sex with random guys has never made me nervous, but Eamon isn't exactly random. He's soon to be my best friend's brother-in-law. If tonight goes badly, the rest of the week could be uncomfortable.

"My ex-girlfriend fancied herself a social media influencer," Eamon says.

"And you kept everything? That's a pretty baller move."

He laughs. "I own the flat, I paid for the furniture. Every few weeks, Sophie emails, asking when she can stop by to collect her throw cushions and plants. My answer is always the same. Never."

"Wow."

Eamon nods as he chews a bite of kebab. "Yeah."

"How long ago was this?"

"Six months, so . . ." He clears his throat. "Bit of a dry spell."

That tiny pause was so thick with vulnerability that I don't know whether to have sex with Eamon or cook him soup—a feeling I do *not* enjoy. I don't do soup for brokenhearted guys.

I don't do relationships. I don't do love. But the kiss in the pub knocked me out of my usual orbit, and the kiss at the front door threatened to send me spinning out into space. My brain knows this is a reckless decision, but the warm, dense desire pooling below my belly is too much to ignore. I glance over at him. "I'll be gentle."

Eamon sucks in an audible breath as his teeth dig into his lower lip. "I can show you to the bath anytime you like."

"Now." The lip thing undoes me, steals my breath. "Now would be good."

He pushes away from the table, leaving a jumble of takeaway paper behind, and takes giant strides across the room, as if bigger steps will get us in bed together faster. He disappears through an archway. I catch up to him in a narrow hall as he opens the bathroom door.

"Standard shower. No special tricks," Eamon says. "I'll um—I'll be in the bedroom." What he leaves unsaid, but I hear anyway, is *hurry*.

Chapter 3

I've been traveling for most of my life—first with my dad, then on my own. After so many years, so many miles, I've learned what's important and what's a waste of space. I carry only what I need. I wear wool layers that can go weeks without washing and my shower regimen consists of a single honey oatmeal bar, but I always pack something sexy—in case a handsome Irishman might be waiting for me in his bedroom.

Wearing my favorite black lace bralette and matching underwear, I'm clean and barefoot as I walk down the hall to Eamon's room. From the doorway, I see him lying on the bed with his eyes closed, idly rubbing his hand along the rise in his navy boxers, and I wonder if he's thinking about me. Heat blooms behind my navel. I try to lean against the doorframe to watch, but the creaky floor gives away my presence. Eamon's hand goes still, and he turns to look at me. "Hi, you."

I step into the bedroom, where I finally see proof of life in the apartment. Terry Pratchett's Discworld series paperbacks lined in a row on the low dresser, clothes piled on a chair, an oddly shaped wooden paddle propped against the wall, and Eamon's bed, a rumpled mess of charcoal-gray linen. "Making sure it still works?"

His laugh is short and quiet. "Something like that."

"Want some help?" I move deeper into the room and climb onto the bed.

Eamon rolls to face me, his hand cupping the back of my head as his mouth covers mine. This kiss is hotter, greedier than the kisses that came before, and we are both breathless when he says, "It's not your *hand* I want wrapped around me."

My words dry up, leaving me with no clever quip or comeback as he eases me back against the mattress. His lips tease down the side of my neck and his fingers curl into the front of my bralette, dragging it down. Eamon's assertiveness is a sexy surprise, and leaving the lights on during sex is one of my kinks. As his mouth wanders into the wide valley between my breasts, my back arches with anticipation. His tongue circles my nipple and I gasp. He lingers there. Kissing. Licking. Catching the hardened peak lightly between his teeth. Until my nerve endings are so lit up, I could illuminate the room. Until I hear my own voice, pleading for more.

Eamon's hand skims down my stomach and dips into the front of my underwear. His touch is gentle as he eases me open, but when his fingertips graze my sweet spot, my hips buck and a passioned cry escapes me. "Oh, fuck. *Eamon.*"

His low laugh rumbles around my nipple, sending a hot frisson of need straight to my core. His fingers begin to move in lazy circles and my head drops back against the pillow. At once, my senses begin the spiraling climb toward release. Eamon takes me higher, his fingers moving faster, until my body tightens to the breaking point.

His hand goes unexpectedly still.

My breathing is ragged. My heart feels like it might burst out of my chest. I'm aching with unfulfilled need. My fingers are clenched around thick handfuls of bedsheets. And I should be embarrassed by the way I whimper when his body shifts away from mine.

Eamon hooks his fingers into my underwear, and I lift my hips as he eases them down. He tosses them on the floor before settling back on the bed, his breath warm on my skin as he kisses my inner thigh.

"You don't have to—"

His tongue sweeps over the spot where his fingers had been, and my words devolve into a low, guttural moan. My hips surge upward. The dizzying ascent begins again, and anything I try to say spills out as incoherent, needy sounds. I've had sex with men who couldn't find a clitoris with a GPS, and others who only cared about their own needs. But Eamon is unhurried, his tongue relentlessly soft against my most sensitive skin. The intensity is almost too much to bear. When his gaze travels up my body to meet mine, I come utterly undone. My eyes fall closed. My hips writhe against his mouth. My legs tremble. His name pours out of my throat as my body quakes with release.

Tiny aftershocks ripple through me as Eamon removes his boxers and reaches into the nightstand drawer. As he sits back on his heels and unrolls the condom, he flashes me a smug little grin, obviously pleased with the bone-melting effect he has on me, and I crave him again. Eamon positions his body over mine, leaning down to kiss me with my taste still lingering on his lips. And when he's finally inside me—when it's not my *hand* wrapped around him—I feel a fleeting, perfect moment of relief.

"Jaysus," he breathes, his beautiful face etched with pleasure. "I could die right now. That would be fine."

My own self-satisfied smile spreads across my lips as I wrap my arms around him and walk my fingertips down his spine. Eamon shudders, then groans as my hands grip his ass and pull him deeper into me. He responds in kind, slowly rocking his hips.

Teasing me in the most delicious way.

Our bodies begin moving together and time is suspended. The world falls away, leaving the sound of his skin against mine. Raspy moans. Sharp gasps. Primal grunts. With each stroke, shivers race toward my center. I want Eamon to come with me, but I don't know how to stop myself from tumbling over the edge. My orgasm breaks over me like a wave.

"Oh, fuck. Yes," he groans, as my body convulses around him. He braces his hands on either side of my head, his pace quickening, thrusting deep. Until his head falls back and the sound that roars out of his mouth is the most glorious of hallelujahs.

Eamon collapses against me, nuzzling his face into the side of my neck. We are both short of breath and slick with sweat, and his weight feels like the only thing tethering me to the earth. Like I could float out the window into the Dublin night. My brain drifts on a sea of postorgasmic bliss.

"Congratulations," I say.

"For what?"

"Your dry spell is broken."

He laughs as he falls onto his back. "Imagine if you hadn't kissed me in the bar."

"Imagine if we'd met at the airport like we were told." I roll onto my side and rest my chin on his chest.

"Right now, we'd be in Tralee, and I'd be preparing to sleep in my childhood room with my brother. It's a guest room now, so there's only one bed," he says. "No offense to Keane, but I'd much rather share a bed with you."

I smile and he ruffles my hair in a way that's tender and affectionate.

"What's the family home like?" I ask.

"Four walls on the outside. Fairly standard," he says. "But inside was pure chaos, especially when all seven of us lived at home."

"That sounds fun."

Eamon side-eyes me. "The reason I live in Dublin is so I can control how often I see my family. I love them dearly, but I was born to be an only child."

Maybe that's why his apartment is so plain and orderly, I think, but then I look around his messy bedroom and my theory doesn't hold water. I don't know him well enough to understand what makes him tick, and maybe it's best not to try. Just because we had sex doesn't mean we have to bare our souls.

"Listen," he says, lifting his head to kiss me. "I'm starting to marinate in this condom. I need to go have a quick wash."

While Eamon is in the bathroom, I rearrange my bralette and put on my underwear before venturing to the kitchen for a drink of water. I find a set of clean linens in a built-in cabinet at the end of the hall and change the sheets. I'm a little embarrassed by the size of the wet spot, but sweet baby Taddy Finnegan, that man is a marvel with his tongue. Finally, I grab a tank top from my backpack, and when Eamon comes out of the bathroom, I enter. He stops me in the doorway with a toe-curling kiss that suggests this isn't a one-and-done kind of night. And I have no complaints about that.

Except when I return to the bedroom, Eamon is fast

asleep. It's not terribly late, but he doesn't stir when I switch off the light. I don't need postcoital cuddling. If I've learned anything in this life, it's that everything is temporary. Don't get attached; it doesn't last. Which is why it's perplexing that I'm kind of . . . disappointed.

My system is still running on Fort Lauderdale time, so I leave him there and walk through the living room to open the French door leading out to the balcony. A switch beside the door illuminates a string of twinkle lights, which cast their soft glow on an outdoor sofa, a small coffee table, and a climbing trellis covered with star jasmine. The sweet scent drifts on the cool night air as I step out onto the balcony and peek over the metal railing. The street below is quiet, and all the shops are shuttered. I imagine the nights are more bustling on the weekends, but tonight it's peaceful.

I check my phone and there's a message from Stella. HE FORGOT YOU WERE GOING TO IRELAND, BUT HE REC-OGNIZED YOUR PICTURE. HE SAID HE LIKES YOUR HAIR SHORT.

Dad met Stella about a decade ago, when she was out walking her American Foxhound, Harvey. The dog's leash got hopelessly tangled around the legs of Dad's chair on the out-door patio of a coffeeshop and the big, ungainly dog nearly toppled the chair. It was the perfect romance novel meet-cute. Love at first sight. And even after finding out that forever was not in the cards, Stella has stuck by him. I love her for not trying to mother me, and I love her for taking care of Dad, but texts like these stir up complicated feelings. Sometimes I resent that I'm the one he sent away.

I put the phone down without responding, but it lights up suddenly with a ringtone that signifies an incoming video call. The only person I ever FaceTime with is my dad, and those calls are sacred.

His face appears on the screen. As always, his gray hair is a throwback to the seventies, and he's wearing his black-rimmed glasses. I smile, happy to see him. "Hiya, Biggie."

"How's my favorite girl?"

"A little jet-lagged, but otherwise okay," I say. "How are you?"

"Oh, you know," he says. "My brain is like an out-of-control TARDIS, so I never know where I'm going to land, but any day I recognize you is one for the books."

I feel a catch in my chest. "Are you doing anything interesting today?"

"Ugly Louie is on his way over," he says. "We'll probably talk shit and maybe I'll have him give me a tattoo."

Louie Ferrari has been his best friend since Biggie landed in Fort Lauderdale decades ago. Louie's retired from the auto repair business, but apparently, he's still doing tattoos.

"Over my dead body," Stella says, her face appearing on the screen.

Her lipstick is scarlet, and her hair is styled like Jane

Fonda, circa 2018. Stella is a lot, but Dad loves her madly. I love her too. And I hope age will be as forgiving to me as it's been to her.

"Hi, honey," she says to me. "How's Anna? Is she nervous about the big event?"

"I haven't seen her yet," I say. "Eamon picked me up from the airport, but we're not heading to Tralee until tomorrow morning."

I hear a knock at the door and Biggie does a quick glance away.

"Louie's here," he says. "Love you, kid."

"I love you, too."

When he's gone, I ask Stella how he's really doing. "Today is a good day, but they're not as frequent as they used to be, honey. Some days he doesn't recognize me, and he gets so angry that I'm a little afraid. He's always been a big softie, but on those days he's just . . . he's just not himself."

I don't know what to say. This is the reason Biggie sent me away. This is the reason I don't go home. I swallow down a lump.

"But enough about that," Stella says. "Is Eamon the brother?"

"Yes."

"Is he as hunky as Keane?"

I'm laughing as I look up to find Eamon standing in the doorway that opens from his bedroom onto the balcony, wearing only his boxers. His shoulders alone make me want to climb him like a tree. His eyebrows raise as he waits for me to answer Stella.

"He's hunkier."

"Well, I'll be looking forward to the pictures from *this* wedding," she says. "I'd better go supervise the boys. No telling what Biggie might get up to while Louie is here. Have fun!"

"I will," I say. "Bye."

She waggles her fingers at me, and then she's gone.

Eamon steps out and sits close enough to me that our bodies touch, his skin warm in the cool air.

"So, how much of that did you hear?"

"Most," he says. "Do you want to talk about it?"

"No."

"Are you okay?"

"Jet-lagged, mostly," I say.

"Whiskey or weed?"

I laugh. "Whiskey would be great."

"I'll be back."

Eamon disappears through the living room door, and he's gone for several minutes, but when he finally returns, he's carrying mugs instead of whiskey glasses. One mug is stoneware with a white bottom and muted blue sides. It looks handmade. The other has the word *gobshite* printed around the belly.

"A housewarming gift from Keane," he explains, handing

me the nicer stoneware mug. It's warm, and the aroma drifting up is sweet.

"Hot chocolate?"

Eamon shrugs one shoulder. "Cocoa with a shot of Jameson always helps me sleep."

"Thank you."

"It's nothing."

I take a sip, then sit back against the couch. "Your balcony is magical."

"Sophie and I had a massive blowout over the balcony because she wanted to mount a wooden grid and hang little woven baskets of jasmine," Eamon says, propping his feet on the coffee table. I do the same, and he rests his big toe against mine. "I casually pointed out that it's a climbing plant not meant to be contained, and she ate my fecking head off. When I reminded her that we lived in a flat in Dublin and not in an Instagram account . . . well, that may have been the last straw."

"Look, I've only known you a few hours, so take my opinion for what it's worth," I say. "But this is *your* apartment, and it looks like no one lives here. As much as I appreciate you keeping her boring shit out of spite, box it up. Tell her if she wants it, she'll find it out back beside the garbage can or whatever you call it here. And because I'm one hundred percent that petty bitch, leave a bouquet of jasmine on top of one of the boxes."

I glance over at Eamon, who's gone goggle-eyed as he stares at me. I can't tell if he's registering shock or awe, until a smile spreads across his face. His shoulders shake with quiet laughter. "I can't decide if that's genius or evil."

"It's a little of both."

We fall silent as we drink our hot chocolate.

"You know, I wasn't expecting this." Eamon gestures between us. "But today was pretty fecking great, and you're going to be in Ireland at least a few more days, so . . ."

I nudge him lightly with my elbow. "Only if you promise not to fall in love with me."

"Little chance of that." He takes a sip of cocoa and gives a small sarcastic laugh. "Every time I think a girl is The One, she turns out to be the wrong one."

"That works out perfectly, then," I say. "I'm already the wrong one."

Chapter 4

Eamon's hair is damp, and his eyes are shaded behind black Wayfarers as we set off down the street, carrying our travel bags and insulated mugs of coffee. Wearing jeans and a gray chambray shirt, he has a style that is so put together that if I hadn't already slept with him, I'd think he was not my type. But we're running behind schedule again this morning because he proved in the shower that he is very much my type.

"The thing about parking in the city center is that it comes at a premium," he says, as we round a corner onto a different street. "My flat doesn't have a designated spot, so I lease space in an underground car park. Keeps her protected from the elements."

I can't very well call him out on gendering his car when I drive an old Wrangler named Valentina, but I hope Eamon's not one of those guys who owns a pristine luxury car and freaks out at the slightest speck of dust. He may not have chosen the furnishings in his apartment, but he could afford to buy them, which leaves me mentally guessing that he drives an expensive sports car, like a BMW or Mercedes.

We reach a redbrick apartment building and I follow Eamon down a ramp to a subterranean parking garage. He stops beside a pale yellow Land Rover Series III—an old one with the spare tire mounted on the hood—and I wait for him to bend down to tie his shoe or reposition his duffel bag on his shoulder. Instead, he digs a set of keys from the pocket of his jeans and unlocks the rear door.

My mouth drops open. "Shut the fuck up."

Eamon laughs as he tosses his duffel into the back of the Rover. I stand gawking while he removes my backpack from my shoulder and stows it alongside his bag.

Dad tried for years to find a Series III that we could restore together, but even the ones without running engines were too expensive for us. Eamon's Defender may not be in mint condition, but the restoration work is top-notch. This vehicle did not come cheap.

"Did you do all the work yourself?" I ask.

"Christ, no." He laughs as he opens the passenger door for me. "I bought it like this."

I peer into the back as I climb into the Rover, taking in the two inward-facing side benches, the curved white hardtop that was echoed later in the Discovery series, and all the analog buttons and gears. Dad would go wild for this truck, and I feel a pang of sadness that he's not here to see it. I make a mental note to text him a few pictures when we get to Tralee.

Eamon swings up into the driver's seat and slots the key into the ignition. The engine turns over and over but won't fire. Eamon clicks the key off. He tries a second time. Again, the engine sounds like it wants to start, but won't. He thumps the steering wheel with the heel of his hand. "Fuck."

"It sounds like you're not getting any spark," I say.

"What?"

"It's probably your distributor cap or bad spark plug wires." I open the door. "When was the last time you replaced the cap and rotor?"

"Never?"

In his prime, Dad could be judgmental about people who buy vintage vehicles they don't know how to repair, but I've never agreed with that hot take. I think it's smart to know your way around an engine, but not everyone is mechanically inclined. Eamon may not have the time, skill, or patience for it.

I get out of the Defender and walk around to the front. Unhook the side latches. Prop up the hood. The engine looks clean, but one of the spark plug wires is fried.

"Not a big problem," I say, looking at Eamon through the front window. I drop the hood and brush my hands off on my leggings. "Just a quick trip to the parts store and we'll be on the road before lunch."

Eamon researches the nearest shop, and less than ten minutes later, a cab drops us off at the curb in front of an auto parts shop. Behind the counter is an older man—maybe in his late sixties—who looks like he knows a thing or two about cars. He ignores me and turns his attention toward Eamon. "Can I help you find something?"

"I need a cap, rotor, and plug wires for a 1973 Land Rover Series Three," I answer.

The man's head swivels in my direction, then back at Eamon, seeking either verification or translation. This is not an unusual response. When I was younger, I'd get irritated when I wasn't taken seriously, but I've stopped trying to prove myself to car guys. I know what I know, and their opinions can't change that. But I appreciate it when Eamon shrugs and says, "I'm only going to repeat what she just said, so you may as well go find the parts."

The man disappears down a tall, narrow row, muttering under his breath as he goes. I sidle up beside Eamon. "Just so you know, feminism makes me hot."

He looks at me over the top of his sunglasses. "You knowing how to fix my Rover does the same for me."

"I'll keep that in mind."

He laughs. "I assume that after years of traveling in your Jeep you've learned how to do all the repair work yourself?"

"My dad taught me most of what I know," I say. "But some of it was trial and error. And YouTube videos."

Eamon goes quiet, working his lower lip between his thumb and forefinger, and I can almost see the wheels turning in his head. I have no idea what he's thinking, but his head is somewhere else entirely, and I wonder if he often disappears into his own head or if there's something else going on. He snaps out of his reverie when the auto parts guy returns carrying a stack of boxes, and Eamon reaches for his wallet.

Including the return cab ride, we're back at the parking garage in less than thirty minutes. Between my small Leatherman multi-tool and a small set of socket wrenches Eamon keeps stashed beneath the front seat, I manage to assemble the tools I need to replace the distributor cap, rotor, and all the spark plug wires—even those in decent shape. When I finish, Eamon gets into the cab of the Rover and the engine roars to life.

I climb in beside him and he catches my face in his hands, kissing me hard and fast. "You are fecking brilliant."

"That was basic auto repair," I say with a laugh. "You should probably learn it."

Eamon falls silent again, like at the auto supply store. Finally, he says, "Want to hear something funny?"

"Sure," I say, but his tone doesn't suggest that what follows is going to be funny.

"I work for a geospatial information company that creates logistics systems for transportation companies and topographical surveys for urban planning," he says. "We also make digital maps for a multitude of uses. If you need the location of every fire hydrant in Dublin or a subsurface map of all the pipelines in Ireland, we do that."

His job sounds a little dry, especially given my feelings about sitting at a computer all day, but I'm not sure where he's going with this. I remain quiet and wait for him to continue.

"Keane has literally traveled around the entire world. You've visited nearly four hundred national parks in America," Eamon says. "And what have I done? Spent most of my adult life making maps of places where other people go."

"Is that what you wanted to do?"

"At first, yes," he says. "But about three years ago I was promoted to director, which came with a bigger salary. I bought the Land Rover with this grand plan to learn how to do my own repairs, outfit it for overlanding, and travel through Europe, Africa, and Asia. Instead, I ended up with a string of failed relationships, a mortgage, and a job that added more responsibility to my life. To be completely frank, I'm fucking tired of being the responsible one."

I get the feeling there's more to this story. Something that might have to do with having an adventurous younger brother. But I don't want to push at Eamon's bruises.

"Okay . . . so . . . Sophie is out of your life. What's stopping you now?"

His laugh is mirthless. "At the moment? A wedding."

After last night's conversation about Eamon's failure to

find someone to love, I wonder if Keane's getting married is another sore spot, especially after Eamon's comment about always choosing the wrong woman.

"If I asked you to take me to the one place in Ireland you've never been but always wanted to go," I say, "where would you take me?"

"The Wicklow Mountains." Eamon doesn't even stop to consider, which means he's already spent a lot of time thinking about the things he would do, if given the opportunity.

"How far is that from here?"

"Roughly an hour."

"An *hour*? And you haven't been yet? That's unacceptable," I say. "The wedding isn't happening until Saturday. Let's find a camping supply store and buy what we need. Take me to the Wicklow Mountains."

Eamon doesn't respond as he puts the Land Rover in reverse and backs out of the parking spot. He drives up the ramp, out of the garage, and a few minutes later parallel parks in a spot opposite his apartment building.

"Come with me," he says, taking my hand.

We run across the street and ride the elevator in silence to the top floor. I follow Eamon through his apartment to the second bedroom, where he flings open the closet door. Inside, there is a towering pile of camping gear—tent, sleeping bags, air mattresses, camp stove, 12-volt cooler-style refrigerator, plastic bins filled with cookware, utensils, and other small accessories. Eamon has supplies for backcountry camping as well as car camping.

"You must have spent a small fortune on all this stuff," I say.

A grin creeps up one side of his cheek and that dimple appears. "This may have been the penultimate straw."

I laugh. "I'm shocked."

"Sophie and I were completely incompatible."

Incompatible seems like an understatement, but I keep the opinion to myself. "Sounds like it."

Eamon rubs his hands together, practically crackling with excitement. "What do we need to bring?"

"Are there campgrounds?"

"No campgrounds. Wild camping only."

I laugh. "Diving straight into the deep end, huh?"

"Go big or go home."

We drag everything out of the closet, and I pare the equipment down to the basics for backcountry camping. I don't know the specific rules for Ireland, but I'm sure they're not much different than in the United States. Leave no trace. Distance yourself and your waste from roads, trails, and waterways. Make sure you have permission to camp on private land. I prefer car camping because I enjoy being near potable water, electricity, and other people—not to mention sleeping in a hammock strung from my Jeep to any nearby tree—but I keep a small backcountry pack on hand for the rare times I feel like camping in the wild.

Eamon and I distribute the supplies between two backpacks, keeping the loads fair and manageable.

"Nothing makes a hike more miserable than lugging a pack that's too heavy," I explain. "We're not camping for days, so we don't need to carry much."

Once the bags are packed, he changes from jeans and sneakers into a pair of weatherproof hiking pants and expensive-looking trail shoes.

When we return to the Land Rover and Eamon is settled behind the steering wheel, his smile is luminous. Yesterday in the pub he was affable and chatty, but now I see the difference. I never would have guessed that a happy Eamon Sullivan would be another one of my kinks, but that smile warms me . . . *everywhere.*

On our way out of Dublin, we stop at a supermarket.

I hop on the front end of the shopping cart as Eamon pushes it through the sliding doors, earning disapproving looks from some of the elder shoppers.

"With a single-burner camp stove, we can't do anything super involved," I say. "But I've got a recipe I can adapt, and we'll have oatmeal for breakfast with yogurt and your favorite fruit."

We gather all the ingredients, along with a gallon of water for filling drinking bottles and a box of sangria. Eamon eyes the wine. "Who'll be carrying that?"

"Once it's out of the box, it's just a plastic bladder. Easy peasy."

He doesn't respond, but as he stands behind me in the checkout line, he rests his chin on my shoulder. "You're grand, Carla. Thanks a million for doing all this."

"Yeah, well, in case no one has told you lately, you're grand, too."

He kisses my cheek at the same time as he palms my ass, and both gestures make me grin. Already this fling has a different vibe than all the others. I usually prefer emotionally immature men who are just looking for sex because real feelings don't belong in a temporary relationship. But Eamon Sullivan is a genuinely nice person and when we're not having sex, I still like him. And, honestly, I don't know what to make of that.

In the parking lot, Eamon loads the perishables in the 12-volt refrigerator while I hold my breath and text Anna.

> Making a slight detour. We'll be in Tralee tomorrow.

> Should I be worried?

> Not even a little.

Once we're back in the Land Rover, Eamon hands me his phone. It's connected to the stereo, one of the few modern upgrades to the old-school dashboard. "Play some music."

I open one of his music apps, follow my account with his, and cue up one of my favorite road trip playlists. Eamon glances at the playlist title on the dashboard screen and laughs. "I needed that."

"Needed what?" I ask.

"Joyful shit."

Chapter 5

Wind whips through the open windows of the Land Rover and my feet are propped on the dashboard as I list the countries I've visited. Dad and I started out touring the United States, but as I got older and more self-sufficient—especially after I learned how to drive—we broadened our horizons. "Canada, Mexico, Puerto Rico, Guatemala, Belize, Honduras, Costa Rica, Netherlands, Belgium, France, Germany, and Denmark with my dad. On my own, I've been to Finland, Montenegro, and Nicaragua."

"Three vastly different places," Eamon says.

"I closed my eyes and threw a dart at a map."

"Seriously?"

"Nicaragua was pretty cheap," I tell him. "I rented a beach casita for four months, cooked all my own meals, and went surfing every morning at dawn. Montenegro, I backpacked through and spent the last month in a one-room apartment overlooking the beach at Budva. Finland was super expensive, so I decided to rent a cabin as far north as my budget would allow and hang out under the Northern Lights for a couple of weeks."

"What if the dart had landed somewhere there was political unrest or war?" Eamon asks.

"A pinhole in a map isn't a binding contract. I re-throw the dart."

He laughs. "Fair enough, but how, um—how do you afford to travel so much?"

"I take every shift I can get from November through April when the snowbirds are in town," I explain. "If someone takes a sick day, I work it. I volunteer for double shifts. I kiss our customers' asses, eat a lot of cheap meals, and sublet crappy apartments in sketchy neighborhoods. It's exhausting, but it makes the rest of the year special."

"Do you ever worry about the sustainability?"

"What do you mean?"

"Is this how you picture your life at, say, sixty-five?"

I laugh a little. "You'd be shocked by how many old servers and bartenders are still working in Fort Lauderdale, but I get your point. Maybe someday I'll want a more financially stable life, but I tend not to think too far into the future."

Eamon doesn't respond, but again I feel like I can see his mind at work, and it all starts making sense. He's inserting himself into a life like mine, trying it on for size. He's wondering if he dares to follow the dream that he shared with me this morning in the parking garage. Whether by nature or nurture, Eamon Sullivan is less impulsive than Keane. Eamon's desire to go is strong, but he also seems to want assurance that he can safely return. It's almost like he's waiting for someone to give him permission.

"You wouldn't have to worry about finding a job," I say. "Computer skills will always be in demand. I've met graphic artists and Web designers who work on the road. I'm the one who's going to have to find myself an old millionaire and make his death look like an accident."

Eamon laughs. "Why do I feel like you could successfully do that?"

"A little evil, a little genius." I flash him a grin.

I shift in my seat, leaning back against the door and stretching my legs across the middle seat. I poke my sock-covered big toe against his thigh. He reaches down and rests his hand on top of my foot, giving it a gentle squeeze. Anna told me the Sullivans are a physically affectionate bunch, and I didn't really understand what that meant. But whenever Eamon reaches for my hand or kisses my cheek, it's like a little reminder: *Hey, I'm thinking about you right now.* Most guys aren't that sincere. At least not in my experience.

Around us the landscape has grown less populated since we left Dublin. Wilder. Greener. And the road begins to climb into a small range of mountains that are more Appalachian than Rocky, more rolling hills than snowcapped peaks. The Wicklows are covered with grassland, threaded with thick, beautiful ribbons of purple heather and yellow gorse. Eamon turns the Rover into an empty gravel parking lot beside a small wood and cuts the engine. We apply sunscreen and double-check our packs to make sure we have everything we need before Eamon locks all the doors.

"Ready?" I ask, hooking the backpack over my shoulders.

"Well beyond," he says, taking my hand and smiling like he's never been more ready for anything in his life. "Feeling really fecking excited and rather embarrassed that I owned a closet full of camping equipment I've never used."

I'll never get to reexperience my first time walking in the woods with Biggie. It was at De Soto National Forest, and I remember him holding my hand on the trail until I felt ready to let go. He always let me be a child, but never talked down to me. I smile at the memory, my heart clenching a little, and at Eamon.

"You're starting now," I say, feeling excitement *for* him. "That's really all that matters."

The first section of the trail passes through a pinewood that's beautiful and eerie. It feels like we're utterly alone. So vast, yet so intimate, like we're the only two people on earth. The trees soar toward the sky, but the canopy is so dense that hardly any sunlight filters through. The lower branches of the trees are spiky and bare, and it feels like something sinister could be lurking among them. But in the places where the sun breaks through, the trunks, the ground, and the rocks are wrapped in moss, turning everything green.

"It feels like we're in Middle Earth," I say.

"There are some who believe Ireland was Tolkien's inspiration for the books," Eamon says. "But others say he never visited the country until after the books were written, so who can say for sure?"

The mention of Tolkien takes me back to when I was about five or six. Dad had already discovered that it took way too many picture books each night to get me to settle down for sleep, so he started reading *The Fellowship of the Ring* aloud. Even with Biggie paraphrasing that dense Tolkien prose, I couldn't understand all the words, but I was enchanted by the idea of elves and hobbits and orcs.

One night, when he was reading about the half-elf Elrond and his daughter, Arwen, I asked my dad why Arwen's mother wasn't in the book.

"Celebrían was captured by the orcs, and they hurt her," he said. "Even after she was healed, she was still very sad, so she sailed to the West, a place where the elves go when they need to feel better."

"Did Arwen ever see her mama again?"

Biggie shook his head. "I'm afraid not."

"Did *my* mama go to the West?"

He was quiet for a long while, and I only realized later it was because he had to collect himself. "Something like that. Your mama went somewhere that would make her feel better."

"Will I ever see her again?"

"Maybe," he said, kissing the top of my head. "But I don't think so."

Eamon is waiting for me to say something, but it's hard to speak with a lump in my throat at the memory of the first and last conversation Biggie and I ever had about my mom. I blink back the tears prickling behind my eyes as I take my phone from a pocket in my leggings.

"You, um—you should record this moment for posterity," I say. "'It's a dangerous business, Frodo, going out of your door. You step into the road, and if you don't keep your feet, there's no knowing where you might be swept off to.'"

I catch Eamon watching me, a tiny crease between his eyebrows, but it melts away as he grins at my Lord of the Rings quote. "Okay. Let's do it."

I unfold a tiny tripod on a low branch of a nearby tree and mount my phone. I adjust for distance and light before joining Eamon in a spot of sun-touched green. He drapes his arm around my shoulder, and I hook mine around his waist.

"Samwise Gamgee on three," I say. "One . . . two . . . three."

I press the button on my remote shutter before retrieving the tripod from the tree. As I walk back to Eamon, I sneak a peek at the photo. The green is saturated and rich, and our smiles are genuine. It's such a perfect shot that I consider uploading it to my Instagram account. Until I remind myself that I never share pictures of the men I'm sleeping with because the internet doesn't need to know *all* my business.

"This is lovely," Eamon says, nodding his approval at the photo. "Send it to me?"

I shoot him a quick text before continuing down the trail. We walk in the woods for about fifteen minutes more, mostly in silence as we listen to the crunch of our feet over fallen pine needles and the occasional raspy *kraa* from ravens in the trees.

Leaving the woods, the path narrows to a single dirt track through leafy, waist-high ferns, and I drop behind Eamon. Neither of us knows exactly where we're going, but this adventure belongs to him. He should be the first to experience the trail. The wild ferns give way to grassland and dry heath, and the path widens once more. He falls back alongside me as we walk through a small herd of grazing sheep, who watch us with curious eyes. We pass gorse bushes exploding with yellow blossoms, and I stop to take close-up photos.

"God, it's so gorgeous here," I say, running my hand across a tuft of soft purple heather. "I'm sure I'm not the first person in history to want to take off all my clothes and lie in the heather, but I do."

Eamon's laugh is just this side of dirty. "I reckon you're

not, but if you need any help with the clothing removal process, I'd be delighted to lend a hand or two."

I gape at him. "How are you single? Make that make sense."

"I'm typically not so—" He rubs the back of his neck and makes a face like he'd rather have a root canal than finish the thought out loud. "Never mind. I don't know."

I'm curious about what he didn't say, but I don't press the subject. This thing happening between us might be different, but it's still short-term. It's about sex. And if Eamon Sullivan wants to lay me in a field of heather on the side of a mountain in Ireland, like hell I'm going to question it.

The trail begins a steady climb toward the summit. The slope is challenging enough to be a workout on my calves and thighs, but gentle enough that we don't need any special climbing equipment. Two hours from when we left the parking lot, we reach the top of the mountain. The ground at the summit is rockier than below, and a cairn built by other hikers marks the highest point.

I pick up a loose stone, a little bigger than my hand, and offer it to Eamon. "You should do the honors."

"I wouldn't be here if it weren't for you," he says, gesturing toward the pile of stones. "Please."

I scramble up the summit rock and place the stone near the top of the cairn, careful not to displace any of the other stones or topple the whole damn thing, while Eamon takes a picture with his phone. A few seconds later, I hear a ping as he sends it to me.

"Thanks for coming with me," he says, as we slowly walk around the summit, taking in the view. I snap photos of the mountains stretching into the distance, the green valleys that dip between them, and the bright sky laced with puffy white clouds. Below us, an elongated lake ripples as the breeze skims across the surface. Off to the east, the Irish Sea glimmers in the distance.

"What do you think of our wee mountains?" Eamon asks.

"They're beautiful," I say. "But I drove my Jeep through a mountain pass at an elevation about seven times higher than this one, so they're also kind of small."

"No one likes a braggart, Carla."

I laugh. "Hey, I've never overlanded in this hemisphere. Imagine the stories you'll have someday."

"If I go."

"When you go."

Eamon opens his backpack and takes out a sleeve of crackers and a small wheel of hard cheese. We sit on the shady side of the summit, our backs against the rock, munching on crackers and sharing the cheese. We talk about whether the clouds have rain in them and make guesses on how long it will take to find a good campsite. I snap a selfie with the tripod. But it's so peaceful up here above the world that we sit for a long time, enjoying the quiet.

"Do you feel guilty for not going directly to Tralee?" he asks.

"A little," I say. "But Anna's not much of a wedding shower or bachelorette party kind of person, so I don't have much to do, other than offer moral support."

Eamon nods. "I was a bit surprised when Keane told me he didn't want a stag night. He said he's done enough asinine things in his lifetime and has no plans to get married with a hangover or regrets."

"Those two are like . . . binary stars," I say. "Gravitationally bound to each other. Orbiting around their own common center of mass. They don't really need anyone else."

"It's beautiful and terrifying," Eamon says.

I laugh. "Exactly."

"If my history is any indication, I may be better off adopting a kitten than trying to find a soul mate and—" He breaks off before continuing with a self-deprecating laugh. "And this conversation has officially taken a turn for the pathetic." He stands and brushes off his hands. "We should keep moving before I make an utter Muppet of myself."

I watch him as he puts away the food, wondering how he's managed to slip through so many nets. It makes sense that Keane was single for a long time. He's basically the male version of me. But Eamon is charming and sincere and exceptionally good at sex, so either he's a terrible judge of character . . . or there's something wrong with him. And I can't help wondering which.

The trail continues down the opposite side of the mountain toward the lake. As we descend, a whole other set of muscles gets a workout. By the time we reach the edge of the lake, we're both winded and sweaty in a not-at-all-sexy way. I drop my pack, ready to wade out into the blue. "That water looks so inviting."

"Wait until we get to the campsite," Eamon says. "If the spot I've got marked on my GPS is as good as I suspect, there will be a much more private place to dip your toes."

I shrug on my backpack with a sigh, and we follow the shore to where a narrow, rocky river feeds into the lake. The sound of water splashing over stone is like music as we walk along the riverbank to a spot where sandy shoals make for a perfect place to cross. We ford the river and continue for about another mile, until finally Eamon leads us through a small stand of trees to a grassy clearing beside the river. It's secluded, and there's a miniature waterfall in the river, with a small pool below. It's not a swimming hole like De Soto, but it might be deep enough for a soak. The best part is that on the sunny side of the clearing is a patch of flowering heather. Eamon gives me a meaningful look and I smile back, knowing we're thinking the same thing.

Chapter 6

Before I do anything else, I submerge the sangria in the river beside our campsite. Eamon unpacks the tent, which takes only a few minutes to set up. We inflate the camping pads and roll out the lightweight sleeping bags.

"I think we could probably get away with a small fire," he says. "We're clear of the trail and protected by trees, so there's little chance of being seen."

"Sounds good to me."

We set off in separate directions to gather firewood and kindling, and by the time the fire is going, I've worked up even more of a sweat than on our downhill trek from the top of the mountain. I strip down to nothing and walk straight into the river.

Ireland is not like Florida. Summer doesn't feel like standing on the surface of a hot griddle. Bodies of water are not gently warmed by the sun to bathwater temperatures. This water is so cold around my ankles that it steals my breath.

I pick my way between the slippery rocks to the shallow pool at the base of the waterfall. The water is about as deep as the shallow end of a swimming pool. I hold my breath and sink until I'm completely submerged, but the water is so cold, I pop right back up. "Jesus Christ."

"Are you trying to get hypothermia and die?" Eamon asks.

"I thought, because I was so sweaty, it might be like a Russian *banya* experience."

He nearly doubles over with laughter. "How did that work out?"

I aim my middle finger at him as I grab my Turkish towel from my backpack. I bought it years ago and it's traveled everywhere with me. I've used it as a blanket while sleeping overnight in airports, as a pillow when there are no pillows to be had, and once as a dress while being chased by police for skinny-dipping in some millionaire's pool in Palm Springs.

"Your turn," I say, using the towel to rub my hair dry. I haven't completely adjusted to life without long hair yet, but I appreciate how much less time it takes to style.

"Thanks," Eamon says. "But no."

I move up close to him and he reaches for my hips, but I gently push his hands away. "I'll be over there in the heather by myself. Come find me when you've washed off the sweat."

He swears a blue streak as he sheds his clothes and ventures into the river, while I spread my towel on the heather. It's not nearly as pillowy or fragrant as I'd imagined, but when I lie back, resting my head among the tiny purple blooms, I feel like a woodland goddess. It feels a little more narcissistic than usual to take a selfie, but this feeling should be celebrated. And the unguarded longing on Eamon's face as he approaches only verifies that opinion.

"I could help you with that, if you like." His voice is hesitant and low.

I've never been especially bashful. My mother was a beautiful woman—and may still be—so I have good genes to thank, and I know my body won't stay this great forever. There might be one or two people who have risqué snaps of me during a drunken game of strip poker in Reno or in a sauna in Finland, but there's no one who has a secret stash of Carla Black nudes.

"This isn't an excuse to take naked photos of you," Eamon clarifies, before I've even had a chance to say anything. "I swear on my own grave."

"You aren't dead."

"I think it's safe to assume that if I were to violate your trust, you'd murder me. Consider it preemptive."

I laugh as I hand him my phone, but as he stands over me with the viewfinder aiming down at my body, I feel vulnerable in a way I normally don't. Not unsafe. Eamon Sullivan isn't remotely menacing, and we've already been as intimate as we could be. But my body—and how I choose to use it—is my armor, and I am more naked than I've ever been. As if my chest is wide open and he can see my issues, tangled up like a ball of Christmas lights.

"Maybe, um—maybe we shouldn't do this," I say, and for a moment I'm unsure if I'm talking about the photo or this fling with Eamon.

He moves immediately, lowering himself to the ground beside me. Close, but not close enough to touch, as he fiddles with my phone. I turn my head to look at him. Eamon smiles, and it does such wonderful things to his face that I can't stop myself from smiling back. The shutter snaps. Without looking at the result, he hands me the device.

"Do you know that you have the faintest freckles on your nose," he asks, as I look at the photo. It was taken on portrait mode, so the focal point is my face and the heather surrounding me. Nothing else. It's probably the best picture anyone has ever taken of me, but it only deepens the feeling that Eamon can see something in me that no one else can. It's exhilarating and scary and I don't know how to respond.

"Thank you," I say finally.

"You're welcome." He inches forward and drops a kiss on the tip of my nose, followed by another on my lips. "You know, I'm still quite cold from the river. I could use a bit of warming up."

My armor snaps back into place and I laugh, slinging my leg over his hips, straddling him. "Is that so?"

His wide smile melts into a more sober expression as he touches one hand to the small of my back, his fingertips warm points of contact against my skin. I rock my hips, rubbing along the hard ridge beneath his soft drawstring shorts, coaxing a groan from his throat. "Yes, most definitely."

The layer of fabric between us creates a dizzying friction. I'd meant to provoke Eamon, but an aching need begins to build where our bodies connect. He strokes his thumb over the bundle of nerves at my center. I pull in a quick, shaky breath that flows back out as a sigh of pleasure. Sparks dance behind my eyelids.

"Look at me." Eamon's voice is low and husky.

Our eyes meet as he teases me with his thumb. The intensity of his gaze is electric to the point of almost being unbearable, and I grind brazenly against him until I feel like I'm going to shatter. This is not like having sex with the lights on. Like earlier, it's as if Eamon is seeing something invisible to everyone else. Feeling suddenly vulnerable, I let my eyes drift shut, wanting to escape into the protection of darkness.

"Look at me," he repeats, his voice softer this time.

I refocus on his gaze and suddenly my climax sweeps

through me. I bite my lip, trying not to cry out, but the full-throated sound rolls across the heath. And all the while my eyes are on Eamon and his eyes are on me.

Until the shuddering subsides.

Until he smiles. "Thank you."

My face grows warm from not knowing how to take any of this. How is this man able to make vulnerability feel good? Why him?

Eamon takes a condom from his pocket. I snatch the foil packet and tear it open while he shoves his shorts down around his thighs. He draws his lower lip between his teeth, watching as I roll on the condom. Watching as I sink down around him, his pupils dilated and dark. I lean forward and his arms come around me, pinning my torso against his as my hips rise and fall. He bites my collarbone. I nip his earlobe. We are not gentle now. We are ravenous, greedy, our mouths clashing as we kiss.

"You are so fucking hot." The words grind out between his teeth. "I can't—"

"Let go."

Eamon holds my hips tight as he thrusts up once. Twice. His head falls back, and he utters a cry that is feral and fierce. I wait for him to collapse, but he rolls us onto our sides and kisses me. His wild energy fades to tenderness, his fingertips resting lightly against the spot where he bit me. He kisses my upper lip, my lower lip. And when he pulls back, his smile is soft. "You are a fucking goddess."

I give a quiet laugh, mostly to myself. "I *knew* it."

●　　●　　●

Eamon rekindles the dying campfire while I set up the tiny propane burner and prepare dinner. My recipe is a deconstructed chicken Marbella—all the prepackaged ingredients tossed into a single pot and cooked only until the couscous is fluffy. It doesn't look fancy, but it tastes hearty and delicious after a day of hiking. Especially when washed down with cups of icy cold sangria.

After we've eaten and cleaned up, Eamon and I lean against a tree, drinking more sangria and listening to the music of the river dancing over the edge of the waterfall, grasshoppers chirping in the heather, and wind softly rustling the leaves above our heads. My whole body is warm and almost humming next to his. He stretches his legs, crossing them at the ankles. "Where was the last place you visited before you came to Ireland?"

"Because of the wedding, I didn't have time to really drive anywhere, so I spent a couple of weeks surfing in the southern part of Mexico," I say. "While I was there, I ate some mushrooms and had a psychedelic vision of a tattoo I ended up getting before I left."

Eamon shakes his head, laughing a little. Like nothing I just said was unexpected. "Which one?"

I pull up the sleeve of my T-shirt and show him the tiny stick-and-poke tattoo on the back of my arm, just above my elbow. There's a sun in the middle with each of the rays transitioning from fire to flowers. He asks me about my other tattoos, and I tell him the stories behind some of them.

"Your father has a friend named Ugly Louie?"

I nod. "And before you ask, he's a regular-looking guy. Neither of them remembers the origin of the nickname, only that they were young, and drugs were involved."

"Which reminds me . . ." Eamon slips his hand into the pocket of his shorts and pulls out a joint. He lights it, takes a drag, and offers it to me.

"My dad's nickname is Biggie," I continue. "His real name is Douglas, but the nickname makes more sense than Ugly Louie because Biggie is six foot five and built like a truck. He's a former high school history teacher, but he looks like a villain in a motorcycle gang movie."

"That's a very specific description."

I pick up my phone and scroll through my photos until I find a recent one of Dad, with his graying 1970s hairstyle, long sideburns, goatee, and black-rimmed glasses. He's wearing a faded brown Flying Burrito Brothers T-shirt with the sleeves ripped off. It's not a stretch to imagine him riding a Harley in black leather or threatening to beat the shit out of someone. Except my dad has never been anything but a softie.

"Okay." Eamon nods. "I see what you mean. He looks like someone who would have loads of interesting stories."

"Thousands." I don't normally talk about my dad, but the sex, sangria, and weed have loosened every part of me. "He grew up in a racist family in central Florida and joined the army to escape them. Ended up in Vietnam. When he was discharged, he used his GI Bill to get a degree in secondary education and taught high school for nearly forty years. Eventually he spent his summers teaching me how to live."

"And your mom?"

"She left when I was five."

"Oh." It's just a single syllable, but leave it to Eamon Sullivan to pack it with empathy.

"She was one of his students. I mean, they didn't have a relationship while she was a teenager in his class," I say. "But when she went back to Fort Lauderdale for her five-year reunion, they . . . connected. She got pregnant with me, and they married quickly, but it only took her a few years to realize she didn't want to be tied down with a kid and a husband who was nearly twenty years older."

"That's . . ." Eamon trails off, either at a loss for what to say or taking the time to gather appropriately sympathetic words for my parents' train wreck of a marriage. One of the reasons I rarely talk about my parents is because it makes them both sound like bad people. But Dad didn't groom my mother or wait around for a teenage girl to become legal. She was a name on a roster, an occupied chair in his classroom, until the night her reunion class invited their favorite teacher to join them for drinks. Was she too young for him? Definitely. Should he have made a different choice? I wouldn't be here if he had, so my objectivity is clouded, but yeah, probably.

"A series of unfortunate events and questionable life choices," I say, filling in the blank.

"I'm sorry about your mom."

"Don't be." I poke at the fire with a stick, sending up sparks. "If I had the chance to rewrite history and make her stay, I wouldn't do it. My dad's not perfect, but when she lost interest in being my mother, he did his best to be a good father."

"It sounds like he gave you an idyllic childhood."

"We did everything together."

"You're fortunate," Eamon says. "When you come from a family of seven, you rarely get individual attention from your parents, unless you've misbehaved. Which might explain why Keane was such a troublemaker."

We fall into silence, but it's companionable. Eamon refills our cups and tethers his phone to a small speaker clipped to the strap of his backpack. He hands me the phone. "You're better at this than I am."

I search through my playlists until I land on one filled

with my dad's favorite songs, mostly from the seventies. We argued so often over his bullheaded theory that music made after that decade was all garbage.

"Oh, come on," Dad said once. "Eighties hair bands were all gimmick, no substance."

"I don't know. Some of those bands are still touring, even though the one remaining original member is the bassist no one cared about," I pointed out. "They have die-hard fans."

"That's because nostalgia is a helluva drug."

"Says the guy still clinging to the seventies."

Smiling at the memory, I put the playlist on shuffle and the first song is "Dancing in the Moonlight" by King Harvest, a song too infectious not to get up off the ground. Dad might have been wrong about good music being made after the seventies, but there *are* a lot of great songs from his era.

I extend a hand to Eamon. "Dance with me."

He lets me haul him to his feet and starts shimmying his shoulders and gyrating his hips, and I realize I'm witnessing his fatal flaw.

"For someone so good at sex, you are a terrible dancer," I say, as his elbows flail in a funky chicken maneuver.

He leans in close to my ear, his voice low. "Would you rather I be better at dancing?"

Shivers zip down my spine, but I laugh them away. "Carry on."

We frolic around the campfire, gyrating like gazelles having seizures. Leaping. Twirling. Singing along at the top of our lungs. Eamon chose the campsite so we wouldn't be seen, but if there's anyone nearby, they can surely hear us.

When the song fades, Eamon grabs our cups and we down them quickly as the opening strains of "Mr. Blue Sky" by ELO fill the air. He catches my hand, and we do our best at old-timey jitterbug dancing, laughing all the way through the song. And when the playlist shuffles to "September" by Earth, Wind & Fire, we break out our sweetest disco moves. By the end of the third song, we're both breathless and grinning.

"You're good *craic*," Eamon says, dropping to the ground. He props his hands behind his head and tilts his face toward the stars. I lie beside him. Except for a few thin, wispy clouds, the dark sky is riddled with stars. "And this is a great playlist."

I explain how it's made up of Biggie's favorite songs and how we used to fight over music.

"He would always end our arguments by asking me to play 'that one song by the band that doesn't suck' but never specified which song or which band," I say. "So, I'd choose something random like Pearl Jam or The Killers or . . . okay, Biggie pretended to hate Bastille the same way I pretended to hate The Flying Burrito Brothers, so I'd play 'Pompeii.' And he would just smile and say, 'Yeah, that's the song I meant.'"

There's a bittersweet note in my voice that I can't conceal, and I don't want to talk about my dad anymore. Memories like these are fine, but I don't want to think about how there are days when I'm video-chatting with a stranger who doesn't recognize me. I roll onto my side and study Eamon's profile. Straight nose. Strong jaw. A chin that's not weak or too square. His lower lip is like a goddamn pillow. No one should be allowed to be this handsome.

"Stop staring at me," he says, keeping his eyes fixed on the night sky.

"I was only noticing that your ears kind of stick out."

"Fuck off."

Laughing, I lean in close, like I'm about to say something sexy. Instead, I jam my tongue in his ear in a decidedly unsexy way.

"Fecking hell!" He sits bolt upright, pawing at his ear. "That's disgusting."

"Really? After some of the places my tongue has been, your *ear* is a bridge too far?"

Eamon's laugh rings out. "I really need someone—a therapist, perhaps—to explain to me why this entire exchange has made me hard as a brick."

"That's the whole point of a fling." I stand, brushing the grass off my legs as the playlist shuffles to the Lord Huron cover of "Harvest Moon" by Neil Young. "Nothing kills the mood faster than overthinking."

Eamon gets to his feet and unexpectedly sweeps me into his arms. With one hand resting on my lower back, he holds me gently against him. This song is my favorite. It's one I find almost unbearably romantic, and I almost pull away, so the melody doesn't attach itself to the memory of this man. But Eamon twirls me gently out and brings me back, and when I glance up at his face, I find him watching me with the barest hint of a smile playing across his lips. I could ask him what he's thinking, but I don't want to spoil the moment. Instead, I rest my head against his shoulder, and as we sway together in the light of the dying embers, he sings softly to me about strangers, lovers, and love under a harvest moon.

When the song ends, Eamon takes my hand and leads me into the tent. His mouth finds mine, but his kisses are languid and sweet. He removes my clothes with the same un-hurried pace, exploring each revealed part of my body as if it's a new discovery. And when we're finally sated and spent, his chest pressed against my back, I try to understand how anyone could let a man like Eamon Sullivan go.

Chapter 7

Eamon is quiet as we drive out of the Wicklow Mountains, heading down a narrow road toward the highway that will take us to Tralee. Despite the oatmeal turning out a little lumpy, he was fine during breakfast and even whistled a nameless little tune as we broke camp. We followed a different trail through the valley, around the opposite side of the lake and through another pinewood that stretched along the bank of a second river. Eamon slung me over his shoulder like a sack of grain as he forded the shallows of the river, then kissed me after setting me on my feet. But since leaving the parking lot, he's been kind of lost in his own head.

I turn down the music. "Are you okay?"

"Ireland isn't well known for the kind of off-road tracks you have in America," he says. "They exist, and we do have a few somewhat challenging green lanes, but you'll not find anything like Moab or the Rubicon Trail."

I poke his thigh with my toe, curious where this is going. "Both of which I've done, by the way."

"Yes, well, no one asked you." Eamon grins, and the tension in my chest eases. "Several months ago—before Sophie and I split—I was having difficulty sleeping. So, one night I was poking around online and found the coordinates for a disused railway line in Donegal. I was intrigued because I hadn't taken the Rover off-roading yet, and I thought perhaps it would be an interesting place to begin."

A white tradesman's van approaches from the other direction and I white-knuckle the door handle as the side mirrors of the two vehicles nearly kiss when we pass on the narrow road. There are roads like these all over the world and I've navigated a few, but it's different when you're in the passenger seat and have no control over the driver—or the vehicle coming at you. I glance over at Eamon, but he's completely unaffected.

"I showed Sophie a video and asked if she'd like to go for a drive in the country," he says. "She was happy enough posting filtered photos of a pretty pastel yellow Defender on her Instagram but turned up her nose at the idea of actually going off-roading."

"I already wasn't her biggest fan," I say. "But now . . . she's dead to me."

Eamon laughs. "And to me."

"How far is this railway from here?" I ask, thinking he wouldn't have mentioned it if he wasn't considering a run.

He focuses on the road through a series of juddering bumps. The all-terrain tires do their job, but old Land Rovers—not unlike old Jeep Wranglers—were never meant for creature comfort. I grip the doorframe again, until the pavement smooths out.

"About four hours," Eamon says.

"And from there to Tralee?"

He considers. "Five, maybe six hours."

Anna is not the Bridezilla type. She's not going to fire me as her maid of honor, or even as her best friend. I don't want to play fast and loose with her goodwill, but the chance to do a little off-roading in Ireland—especially with a good-looking Irishman behind the wheel—is too tempting to deny. "Okay, but it's your turn to break the news to Anna and Keane."

He pulls off the road along the edge of a grassy meadow and puts his phone on speaker as it rings. Keane answers. "Howya? Are you on the way?"

"Ah, I'm grand, yeah. But we're going to be a little later than expected. Last-minute, unavoidable work thing."

"Eamon." Keane's voice drops, low and serious. "You're my best man and you've got the fucking rings."

"It'll be fine," Eamon says. "We'll be there tomorrow afternoon."

Keane is one of the chattiest people I've ever met, so his

silence is oppressive. He's also the kind of guy who would realign the planets to make Anna happy, and I start to have second thoughts about this off-road plan. I'm about to tell Eamon we should bail when Keane exhales heavily. "Mom has already been giving out to me about you being late. She didn't appreciate it when I told her your whereabouts are not my responsibility, and I don't know how much longer I can hold her off."

"Now you know how it feels to be me," Eamon says.

"What?"

"Nothing. Forget it. I swear to you, we'll be there tomorrow."

"Fine," Keane says, but his tone makes it very clear that nothing about this is fine. "Just . . . please don't fuck this up."

"I won't," Eamon says.

"You didn't tell me you have the rings," I say, after Keane disconnects.

"Would we be on our way to Donegal right now if I had?"

"Maybe not."

"Well, then."

"Okay. Let's do this." I set up the navigation coordinates of the disused railway, and when we reach the road that would take us to Tralee, Eamon heads east instead of west. Unlike yesterday, when time felt more limitless, the air of joy has been sucked out of the Rover. Eamon's shoulders climb the back of his neck, and his smile has become a firm, straight line, as if this is less about having fun and more about proving something. But years of traveling have hardened me toward other people's problems, and I remind myself that I came to Ireland for a good time, not to be Eamon's therapist.

I shift my feet down to the floor and slip on my sneakers. "Pull over. I'm driving."

•   •   •

"I honestly believed this was a romantic comedy plot device," I say, peering through the windshield at the tiny rural lane ahead of us, made completely impassable by a flock of sheep.

I try honking at them, but that makes the wooly beasts shuffle nervously around the road, trading places with one another instead of scattering. In Central America, it's not uncommon to swerve around a village dog taking a nap in the middle of the main road, but this lane is bordered by stacked stone fences, making a drive-around impossible.

I throw up my hands in exaggerated frustration. "Now I've missed my train to Dublin, where I was going to propose to my boring fiancé who's been having an affair with his personal assistant behind my back."

Eamon's cheek dimples as he laughs, and I ignore the way my heart kicks at the cage of my ribs like it's trying to break free.

"Welcome to your first Irish traffic jam," he says.

"How long do they stay like this?"

He shrugs. "As long as it takes."

"Long enough for . . ." I trail off, letting him complete the thought for himself.

His eyes widen when he does. "Only one way to find out."

Eamon catapults himself over the seats and tumbles with a thump into the back of the Rover. He's quiet for a beat. Then: "Ow. Zero points to Sullivan for both choreography and technique."

Biting back a laugh, I get out and walk around. By the time I open the back door, Eamon has already removed his shirt. I begin to suggest we don't need to get completely undressed for a quickie in the middle of a deserted country lane, but he has the nicest chest. Just enough definition. Just enough hair. Instead of speaking, I let my eyes follow the trail that disappears into the front of his pants, then glance up at his face. When our eyes meet, it feels like the tiniest spark could detonate the air.

"Fucking hell," Eamon says, as I straddle his hips. "What have you done to me?"

It's unnerving how quickly things seem to escalate between us. How the slightest touch can set me on fire. Holding his face, I lean down to kiss him, teasing my tongue along the inner edge of his upper lip. He growls and slides his hand up my shirt, making me gasp when thumb meets nipple.

It's at that moment—when the sheep, the road, and Ireland itself have completely disappeared from existence—that there's a tap on the window. Eamon's hand goes still, and we both turn to find an old man wearing a farmer cap standing beside the Rover.

"Lane's clear," he says, his voice gruff and matter-of-fact, as if he didn't just witness our absolute inability to restrain ourselves.

Over Eamon's shoulder, I see a solitary sheep lingering at the edge of the road, trying to get in one last nibble of grass before joining the rest of the flock in the opposite pasture. Eamon removes his hand and runs it up through his hair before turning back toward the window, where the farmer is also lingering. "Thank you."

The man raises a hand before trundling away.

Eamon looks at me, the corner of his mouth twitching, and I completely lose it. For the longest time we just laugh. And when our laugh tapers to sporadic giggles, we glance at each other and come undone again. It takes forever to reach the point where we can function without cracking up.

"That was a first for me," he says, pulling his shirt back on.

"Which part?" I wipe the corner of my eye with the side of my palm. "Attempting to have sex in a Defender, the country lane, or nearly getting caught in the act by a farmer?"

"All of the above."

"I guess I can cross those off my bucket list, too."

"Do you actually have a bucket list?" Eamon asks, when we've returned to the front seats.

"Not really. If I want to do something, I tend to do it. And hope I don't die or end up in jail."

"Have you been arrested?"

"Not yet."

"What's the most reckless thing you've ever done?"

"I was camping at the state park on Bahia Honda in the Florida Keys when I met a couple of guys who were there to scatter their friend's ashes in Key West," I tell him. "We did a bunch of tequila shooters, and I woke up the next morning, alone, one island over, in a hammock in someone's backyard. My shoes were missing, and I found a two-hundred-peso note in my pocket that I didn't have the day before. Everything that happened between the tequila and the pesos is a mystery . . . and it bothers me because I was fully clothed and completely dry, but the money was wet."

Eamon stares at me as if I've grown a second full-sized head. "That's so . . . dangerous."

I'm pretty sure dangerous is not the *d* word he was going for, but he's not wrong. I was completely unmoored after Biggie pushed me out of the nest that, for the first few years, recklessness was my signature style. Many of my stories—even some of the best ones—are cautionary tales, but hurtling from one bad decision to the next left little room for loneliness or fear or sadness. And back then, there were days upon days where I hoped I'd die so I wouldn't have to think about Biggie slipping away. So that I didn't see it.

"It was a long time ago, when I was at a really low point in my life." I rush on, leaving no chance for Eamon to ask anything else. "I'm not that wild anymore, although I'm not sure I can be trusted in the back of a Land Rover with you."

He laughs. "It's a shame we were unable to fully test that theory."

"True, but . . ." I start the engine, shove the gear into first, and take my foot off the clutch. "There are lots of miles between here and Tralee."

• • •

We reach the site of Eamon's coordinates in the early afternoon, ending up near a train station that's fallen into disrepair. Since we only planned for one day in the Wicklows, most of our food is gone, but we cobble together a picnic of cheese, crackers, and apple slices. I pour a cup of sangria for myself, but Eamon says he wants to keep a clear head for driving an unfamiliar track.

"How long do you think it will take?" I ask, as we sit cross-legged in the tall grass, facing each other.

"According to my research, the railway line was about fifty kilometers," he says. "I reckon it'll take us about an hour and a half or so, depending on the quality of the terrain. Afterward, we can either wild camp or find a hotel for the night. If we leave in the morning, first thing, we should be in Tralee tomorrow afternoon, as promised."

"Sounds perfect."

"Thank you for humoring me." He gestures toward the Land Rover.

"I'm not humoring you, Eamon. This would be fun even without the sex."

He leans forward, shifts from sitting to crawling, and eases me backward in the grass until he's above me. Eamon kisses me again and again, slowly, sweetly. He makes no move to take things further and after several more kisses, he touches his lips to my forehead and sits back.

"How are *you* still single?" he asks. "Make *that* make sense."

Clouds sail overhead as I lie there a moment, not knowing what to say. Torn between craving more and the impulse to flee. Flight is familiar. Comfortable. But the craving . . . I don't know what to do with it. So, I choose the latter.

"Because no one can catch me."

"Has anyone ever tried?"

Even though I didn't lie to Eamon about throwing a dart that landed on Nicaragua, I hadn't planned to stay there for such a long time. I went because it was cheap, but when I got there, I met Camilo Vega. He was an instructor at one of the local surf schools, and at first, we waved to each other every morning while he was squeezing in a surf session before work. Brief chats came next, followed by hanging out at one of the little beach bars after he finished his lessons for the day. On his days off, we explored the tide pools, soaked in the hot springs, and watched sea turtles hatching at the nearby wildlife preserve. And one night, after we'd both had too much to drink, I took Camilo back to my casita.

He lived with his family up the road from the beach, but during the four months I was in Popoyo, he stayed with me. Nothing on the surface changed. We surfed every morning before Camilo went to work and hung out together when he was done. We didn't name our feelings or make plans, but he called me *mi sol*—my sun—when no one was listening. My wildness subsided, and I wondered if the absence of chaos was the same thing as love.

There's one photo of Camilo on my Instagram feed, a shot of us surrounded by surfers on my last night in Nicaragua, but no one would be able to tell that we were together. He asked me to stay, but I left because that's what I do. I pack all my feelings in the back of a Jeep Wrangler and drive away, just like Biggie taught me to do.

Eamon is studying me, and I realize I've been in my head too long to lie. Camilo Vega was my rehabilitation. Surfing, my meditation. Recklessness traded for a steadier heartbeat.

"Just once," I say, as I get to my feet. I smile, trying to play it off. "He missed."

Eamon doesn't ask anything more, but he keeps darting glances at me that I ignore. As if I might get the urge to explain while we clean up the remnants of our picnic.

We get in the Rover and start off down the old railway line. There are wheel ruts carved into the spaces where the tracks used to run, and grass has sprung up in place of the railroad ties. It's not an especially challenging drive—no boulders or fallen trees to crawl over, or creeks to splash across—but the view is spectacular. The hill-strewn landscape is lush and intensely green, with leafy ferns growing wild beside the trail.

I dig my phone out of my pocket and record a video as we pass through a ravine cut into a rocky hillside back when the railway was built. When we emerge from the other end, the trail continues atop a steep embankment that reminds me of *Murder on the Orient Express*.

"Jaysus," Eamon breathes. "I'd hate to be up here on a windy day."

I peer out my window at the pasture below, where cows are grazing. "That's definitely a long way to fall."

After nearly half an hour, we reach an intersection where the trail is divided by a small dirt road. On the opposite side of the road, the wheel ruts are deeper, awaiting us as mucky little gullies that slow our progress down to a crawl. Eamon maneuvers with care, attempting to straddle the deepest grooves. But the front passenger tire slips into a gully. The center of gravity shifts.

"Fuck," Eamon says quietly.

The sensation of tipping over is like watching a mug topple off a kitchen counter and knowing you're not going to catch it before it hits the floor. Time does a weird dance between too fast and too slow. One moment we're upright, the next we're not. One moment I have a view of blue sky, the next my face is frighteningly close to the muddy gravel of the trail. In between there's the crumpling sound of metal meeting ground. The metallic crunch of something breaking.

And then everything goes still.

Chapter 8

In the dazed silence that follows the crash, I take quick stock of my body. My neck moves. My fingers and toes wiggle. No immediate pain. No visible bleeding.

"Are you okay?" Eamon's panicked voice breaks the silence.

"I'm fine, I think."

"Don't move."

Previous life experience doesn't make *this* experience any less fucked up, so there's a slightly hysterical edge when I laugh. "Where would I go, Eamon? My door is pinned between the trail and a ton of metal."

"I just meant . . . feck, if you're hurt, I don't want you to make it worse."

"I'm not hurt," I say. "But if you're not injured, I'd really like to get the hell out of this vehicle."

He hoists himself up through the open driver's door

window. When he's clear, I unfasten my seat belt and climb out of the Rover. Eamon assists me down to the ground and at once pulls me in for a hug. His arms are tight around me. "I'm so sorry."

Biggie rolled Valentina for the first time when I was eleven years old. We were crawling over a boulder on the Schnebly Hill Road in Arizona when the Jeep tipped backward, then keeled over onto its side. Like this crash, it was a slow-motion roll. Neither of us was hurt and, after some of the other Jeepers on the trail helped winch her upright, Biggie and I finished the run. Granted, we were leaking transmission fluid and Valentina came away with a few new scars, but we earned our trail badge.

"We're not hurt, and I wouldn't be surprised if the only thing you lost is the side mirror," I say, detangling myself from his embrace, despite wanting to sink into it. "Our biggest problem right now is getting the Rover back on four wheels, preferably before dark."

"Maybe this was a bad idea," Eamon says. "Maybe I should—"

"*Stop talking.*"

His eyes go wide, but his mouth goes shut.

"This was nothing." My words come out harsher than I intended, but maybe they're exactly as harsh as they need to be. If Eamon wants to travel the bumpiest parts of the world in this vehicle, he can't chicken out before he's even left Ireland.

He needs the same dose of tough love Biggie gave me so I wouldn't be afraid. "And if you're doing it correctly, this will not be the last time you dump. Get over it."

Everything in the back of the Rover has tumbled to one side. The contents of the cooler are scattered, and sangria is trickling on Eamon's sleeping bag, the bladder having been punctured at some point during the roll. I drop the leaking bag of wine on the ground outside the truck and grab my backpack. We're surrounded by farmland, so there must be a farm somewhere nearby. And where there's a farm, there's usually a tractor.

"Wait!" Eamon says, but I ignore him. I try to open the maps app on my phone, but we're in the middle of nowhere. There's no signal. Zero bars.

"Carla, *stop*!"

The force of his demand halts me in my tracks. I look up. And that's when I see the bull.

He's enormous and black with a lethal-looking span of curved horns. And he's standing about twenty feet in front of me. He's not snorting or pawing the ground like he's about to charge, but his head is low, his nostrils twitching, and he doesn't look pleased to be sharing his land with a pair of two-leggers. Then again, pissed off might be his default expression.

Either way, my heart is pumping double time as I walk slowly backward, my eyes fixed on the bull. His head is like a battering ram and his eyes are endlessly dark. With each step

I take, he takes a step forward, the gap between us never widening, but also never closing. I back up until my back bumps into one of the tires. Eamon is already sitting on the upturned side of the Rover—the highest point. Carefully scaling the dirty, greasy undercarriage, I climb up beside him.

This is not a safe spot—the bull's horns could easily puncture the tires and he could knock us from our perch with very little effort—but there's nowhere else to go. The trail embankment is nearly level with the surrounding terrain, so he could chase us. And I'm not sure we could run fast enough to reach the next closest pasture.

"You had to wear a red shirt today," Eamon says, dryly.

"Yeah, well, encounters with bulls don't normally factor into my daily wardrobe decisions."

He laughs. "Fairly certain it's a myth that bulls hate the color red anyway."

"Fairly certain they hate *everything* and right now, we're probably at the top of that guy's shit list."

The bull walks right up to the exposed belly of the Rover and stops, effectively trapping us. His posture seems more relaxed—at least as relaxed as a half-ton creature with zero chill can be—but he casts a baleful eye in our direction. He stands there for nearly twenty minutes, completely still except for the swish of his tail and the occasional twitch of an ear. Eamon and I don't speak for fear the noise might set him off, but sometime during the wait his hand finds mine and squeezes.

Around us, birds are singing and insects buzzing because our dilemma is not their problem.

When he's finally decided we no longer pose a threat, the bull turns and wanders toward the back of the Rover, where he finds the sangria lying in the grass. He spends a few moments investigating the bladder with his nose, followed by a tentative lick, his tongue nearly the same size as the bag. He must like the taste of the sweet, fruity wine, because he licks it again and again.

Eamon runs a hand down his face. "Jaysus, that can't be good."

"I don't know. Maybe he'll get drunk and fall asleep."

"Or he'll go on an alcohol-fueled rampage and murder us."

"Yeah, but just think about how interesting our obituaries will be," I say, making him laugh. "By the way, I need to pee."

Eamon reaches out and touches my cheek. "It's been lovely knowing you."

"Are you saying you wouldn't throw yourself in front of a bull for me?"

"That"—he lets go of my hand to drape his arm over my shoulder and pull me in for a quick kiss—"is exactly what I'm saying."

"Chivalry is officially dead."

"Be right back," he says, and I wonder where he could possibly go, until he begins lowering himself through the open window. The Rover wobbles and the bull lifts his head, reminding us that he hasn't forgotten we exist, then returns to the sangria. It isn't a big wine bladder, and we drank at least half of it, so I don't think he can get drunk. I hope. Eamon returns with bottles of water and a bag of cheese-and-onion-flavored potato chips.

"If we're going to be here awhile, we may as well enjoy ourselves," he says, handing me a bottle of water. "So, where's a place you haven't traveled that you've always wanted to go?"

Biggie and I talked about going to Iceland, but getting the official diagnosis changed him. I suggested we book the trip while his dementia was still manageable, but he told me his traveling days were over.

"What happened to the family motto?" I asked.

"I've had my good time," he said. "Which is why I'm passing the baton to you."

I never brought it up again, and the idea of going to Iceland without him seems . . . wrong.

"Oh, um, probably Tierra del Fuego," I tell Eamon. "It's been a dream of mine to drive through South America, but I've never been able to afford the shipping fees to get my Jeep there."

"Isn't there a highway?" he asks. "And a bridge over the Panama Canal?"

"The road ends at the Darién Gap, which is basically an impenetrable forest on the border between Panama and Colombia," I say. "Car manufacturers like to film commercials in the Darién Gap to make it seem like their vehicles could navigate that terrain—and they might be able—but in reality, the forest is filled with bugs, snakes, and other things that could potentially hurt you. It's taken me some time to learn, but there's a difference between intrepid and stupid."

Eamon is quiet for a beat, considering. "I read a book once that claimed Bhutan was the happiest country on Earth. I think it's since been toppled from its position by Norway, but I like the idea of visiting a place where happiness is a priority."

"You should go."

He tears open the potato chip bag and offers it to me first. "Someday."

"You recognize the irony, right?"

"It's not that simple."

"Of course it is," I say. "You book the flight. You get on the plane. Prioritize your own happiness, Eamon."

The silence between us feels a little spiky and it's my own fault. Biggie avoided the hard topics whenever possible, but when he told the truth, it never came with sugarcoating. Diplomacy is not the first tool in my interpersonal arsenal, so I often step on people's feelings, usually unintentionally.

"I've lost track of how many people have told me they wish they hadn't delayed their dreams until the timing was right because the right time doesn't exist," I say. "I might end up being the oldest bartender in Fort Lauderdale, still living in shitty apartments, but I won't have any regrets. No one will be able to say I haven't lived."

Except the memory of Camilo Vega resurfaces, quietly reminding me that there's more than one way to live. Reminding me of what I sacrificed for a life on the road. Biggie is safe at home with Stella, and I've heard since from mutual friends that Camilo is married with kids. I'm the one who is still alone, still running.

"I get it," Eamon says. "I do."

I feel like pushing him would just make things worse, so I change the subject. "I noticed the Pratchett books on your dresser. Are you a big reader?"

He lets out a frustrated puff of air. "Let me tell you about the boxes of books I have in my closet that didn't fit our *aesthetic*."

"Sophie?"

He nods.

"Okay, so—" I shift a little to face him. "The bookcase is empty, and your boxes are open and waiting. Which is the first book to get shelved, no questions asked?"

"That's like asking a parent to name a favorite child."

"Yes, but if you are to be believed, Keane is your mom's favorite, so clearly it's not that difficult."

His laugh rings out and the bull snorts. "Sorry, Your Beefiness. Won't let it happen again."

Charmed by his apology to a cow, I lean forward and touch my lips to his cheek. He grins, and as I pull away, Eamon cups the back of my head and gives me a slow, lingering kiss, before considering his favorite book.

"Be warned," I say. "If your answer is *Lolita, Atlas Shrugged,* or anything by Jonathan Franzen, I will throw you off this vehicle with force."

"I thought there were no questions asked," he says.

"All I'm saying is that if you name something that outs you as an immature man-baby, there will be judgment."

His laugh is lower this time, so he won't disturb the bull. "Well, then I hope Gaiman, Adams, and Pratchett meet with your approval, because the first book I would shelve is *Good Omens,* followed immediately by *The Hitchhiker's Guide to the Galaxy,* and the remainder of the bookcase would be needed for the Discworld series, because I own the entire collection."

"Biggie would like you," I say, and I'm hit by a twinge of regret that they'll never have a chance to meet, followed by the sinking realization that there's only ever been one other man that I wanted my dad to meet. This doesn't mean I love Eamon Sullivan—especially not after two days—but it means something, and I'm not sure how I feel about it.

"I'll consider it an honor since you hold Biggie in the highest regard," he says, then—as if he can sense my discomfort—he steers the conversation back. "Do you have a favorite book?"

"Too many to name just one," I say. "But I've read everything by Anthony Bourdain, and my weakness is Regency romance."

Eamon cocks his head. "Bourdain makes absolute sense, but I would never have guessed Regency romance."

"You're not going to throw me off the Rover, are you?"

He scrunches up his nose as if he's deliberating, then flashes a grin. "If we were still upright and on the trail, I might throw you in back and have my way with you, but since we're not . . . did you know that I played hurling in school?"

"No, I did not," I say. "Also, I have no idea what that is."

"It's an ancient game that's a bit lacrosse, a bit field hockey, a bit rugby, and a bit chaos," he explains. "The stick is called a hurley and—"

"Wait. Was that the weird paddle in your bedroom?" I interrupt.

"Yes."

"I thought maybe it was some sort of sex toy."

His eyebrows arch up. "It could be . . . if you're into that sort of thing."

"I mean, I didn't think I was, but now I feel like I'm seeing an Eamon Sullivan no one knows about. And it's kind of hot."

"We really need to stop talking about sex."

I laugh and suggest we play the animal game, a road trip classic that Biggie and I played all the time. One of us would name an animal and the other would use the last letter as the first letter of the next animal. I start with *axolotl* and Eamon follows with *lemon shark,* and I like that. I counter with *kinkajou,* hoping the *u* might throw him off, but he says *urchin.* We go back and forth for a long time, until he chooses *lynx.*

I'm struggling for a response when a fat raindrop splats on the top of my head. Then another drop hits my cheek.

"Oh, for fuck's sake, *seriously*?" I say. "It's not bad enough we rolled off the trail into a bull pasture, but now rain?"

"Ireland," Eamon reminds me, as he scoots over to the window. He climbs down into the Rover and reappears with a bright yellow umbrella, and I wonder if the polka dots were a personal choice or if the umbrella is a leftover from Sophie. It's cute, but not very big, so we huddle close, trying to stay dry as the clouds grow thick and gray, blotting out the sun.

Splattering drops have turned to bucketing rain when we hear the rumble of a motor in the distance. I look up to see a tractor crossing the field, heading in our direction. At the sound of the tractor, the bull ambles away, leaving behind a flattened wine bag—and making it seem like we've been hanging out on top of an upended Land Rover all day for no good reason.

"Oh, now you walk away," I call after him. "I hope you end up medium rare on someone's plate!"

Eamon is laughing when the farmer reaches us. He's about my dad's age, with gray hair and silver-rimmed glasses. His green rubber Wellington boots are caked with mud. He surveys the scene.

"Bit of trouble?" he says, over the growl of the tractor.

"Made a right bags of it," Eamon admits. "We could use some help getting her upright if you wouldn't mind."

The farmer nods. "I'll fetch a strap."

Despite the bull being a black lump in the distance, we stay where we are until the farmer returns with a tow strap. Once we're on the ground, he attaches one end to the tractor, the other to the Land Rover, then accelerates slowly away. The strap goes taut, and with a creaking groan, the Rover pivots first onto two tires, then four, landing with a gentle bounce. The passenger side is covered in dirt, there's a large dent where the body hit the ground, and the crumpled side mirror is dangling by a screw, the reflective part shattered. Eamon looks like he might throw up.

"Can we make sure it runs before you leave?" I ask the farmer, who nods in reply. Then, to Eamon: "Do you mind if I drive?"

"Not at all."

Leaving him beside the tractor, I get into the Rover and slowly maneuver it backward until it's clear of the gully and onto a section of trail that's less bumpy. I sit for a minute, revving the engine and listening. Everything sounds normal, but it's unlikely we came away from the roll without something leaking.

The passenger door sticks when Eamon tries to get in, forcing him to yank it open. "Martin . . . Mr. Gallagher . . .

says to follow him to the house. His wife, Mary, will have supper on, and we're welcome to clean up, share a meal, and stay the night."

Our clothes are drenched, and I have dirt and oil stains streaked across the front of my shirt. And a shared packet of potato chips was not especially sustaining. So I drive off the trail into the pasture, following the tractor in a soggy parade.

"This is very generous considering we made him come out in the rain and let his bull drink our sangria," I say.

"I'd leave out that last bit," Eamon says.

I nod, holding up three fingers like the Girl Scout I never was. "What happens in the pasture, stays in the pasture."

Chapter 9

Martin and Mary Gallagher's house is a traditional Irish cottage with a thatched roof, thick stone walls, and a red front door. It looks like something from a postcard, and I snap a quick photo before Martin steps out in front to open the door. We're barely inside when we're greeted by the scent of stewing meat and by Mary, a woman with a pair of blue cheater glasses nestled in her salt-and-pepper hair.

"Look at the state of you!" she says, ushering us deeper into the house. The stone floor is scattered with worn rugs, and a huge brick fireplace takes up the far end of the main room. The furniture and appliances are a bit dated, but their home is cozy and clean. Inviting. After quick introductions, she says, "I'll show you to the bath and fetch some extra towels."

She hustles me into the bathroom and starts running the water in an old claw-foot tub, then takes a stack of pale yellow towels from a wooden cabinet standing against the wall. "Leave your clothes outside the door so I can wash them."

"You really don't—"

"As soon as you and yer man have finished, supper will be waiting," Mary says in a tone that's both pleasant and final.

Eamon and I take turns, bathing and changing as quickly as possible so we don't delay the Gallaghers' meal any more than we already have. Darkness has fallen outside as we sit down to a dinner of beef with potatoes, carrots, and celery in a dark, savory stew. Before we begin, the others recite a prayer they all seem to know by heart. Having been raised by Biggie Black, I guess I'd call myself agnostic with Buddhist tendencies, so I sit quietly—and hopefully respectfully—while they give thanks.

"Where are you from, then, Carla?" Mary asks, handing me a basket of crusty bread.

I take a slice and pass the basket to Martin. "Born and raised in Florida. Fort Lauderdale."

"We took the boys on holiday to Disney World once when they were young," she says, looking across the table at her husband. "They must have been nine and eleven at the time. I reckon you've been there many times."

When I was growing up, there were kids at school whose families were Disney passholders and went as often as possible. Biggie wasn't strictly anti-Disney, but he thought there were more interesting places to visit, so we never went. Also,

Orlando was a little too close to his hometown for comfort. I shake my head. "I've always wanted to go, though."

I discover that it isn't a lie. I wouldn't trade my summers with Biggie for anything in the world, but for as much as I've experienced, there's an equal amount I've missed. I had friends while school was in session, but alliances shifted over the summer, so I had to reestablish myself every August. Fortunately, I came armed with cool stories.

"What brings you to Ireland?" Mary asks.

"My best friend is getting married," I say. "Eamon's the best man, so he met me in Dublin and we're heading to Tralee."

Martin cocks his head. "Donegal's a bit off the path."

"We're taking the long way 'round." Eamon flashes me a look that's full of pinewoods, moonlight dancing, sheep roadblocks, and sangria-drinking bulls, and I can't keep the smile off my face. "The wedding's not 'til Saturday, so I thought she might like to see a bit of the country."

"Where has he taken you so far?" Mary asks.

"We've been camping in the Wicklow Mountains," I offer. "And we were doing some off-roading on the old railway before the Land Rover took a tumble."

Her eyebrows knit together. In a country steeped in history and littered with old castles, I'm sure our version of sightseeing seems odd. But Mary is too polite to comment. Instead, as we eat, she shares the history of their cottage and stories about their grown sons. Martin is a quiet man who contributes now and then, but his nods and smiles underline his wife's words. There's a steadfast current of love and respect between them that's almost palpable, and a wave of homesickness washes over me.

It's been nearly six years since I've seen my dad in person. Stella keeps me updated on the progress of his dementia and I've shared my adventures with him in video chats, but it's not the same as being wrapped in a Biggie bear hug. Staying in perpetual motion keeps the sadness at bay, but every once in an unexpected while, it sneaks up on me. Looking up from my plate, I see Eamon watching me.

His eyebrows dip in a silent question. *Are you okay?*

No. I don't know. I'm fine. I poke the tip of my tongue out at him and when he smiles, I slide the lock on my feelings and compliment Mary on her stew.

"It's nothing special," she says. "I can give you the recipe, if you like."

I rarely have the chance to cook in a proper kitchen—most of my work is done over an open fire in a cast-iron pot—but I like having recipes for that nebulous someday when I'll live somewhere long enough to have a kitchen. "That would be great. Thank you."

• • •

Mary refuses to let me help clean up the kitchen, so Eamon and I go outside to check on the condition of the Land Rover.

He holds the flashlight while I inspect each part of the engine, checking for cracks or broken pieces.

"You mentioned that your dad taught you how to do auto repairs," he says. "Where did he learn?"

"Vietnam." When Eamon gets quiet, I know the cogs in his brain are turning again. I laugh a little. "But I'm sure there are classes available somewhere in Dublin."

"How can you always read what I'm thinking?"

"Because it telegraphs on your face and in your silences, and because I know what you want."

He palms my ass. "Do you know what I'm thinking right now?"

"Yep." I give him a quick kiss. "Wait here. I'll be back."

The Gallaghers are watching a detective show on TV when I go inside the house. Mary is engrossed, like it may be one of her favorite shows. Martin, on the other hand, looks up as I step into the room.

"I'm sorry to bother you," I say to him. "But do you happen to have any epoxy and maybe some coolant?"

"Sure." A look of relief passes over his face—like maybe he only watches detective shows because Mary enjoys them—and he rises from the couch. I follow him outside, past Eamon, to the barn, where Martin rummages through a cabinet until he finds a tube of J-B Weld and a bottle of antifreeze. "Will these do?"

"Perfectly. Thanks."

I return to the Rover and hand everything to Eamon. "Ready for your first lesson?"

"That . . . was not what I was thinking."

I laugh. "Oh, I know."

"So, what am I learning?"

"How to MacGyver a cracked reservoir tank."

I walk him through the steps: checking that the coolant level is lower than the crack, mixing the epoxy, and applying the mixture to the crack.

"It's that simple?" Eamon asks, lowering the hood.

"We'll top off the antifreeze in the morning, after the epoxy has had time to dry, and eventually you'll need a new reservoir," I say. "But yes, this should hold us until we get to Tralee."

He kisses my forehead. "Thank you. You're grand."

"I know."

Eamon laughs. "Now, about that other thing . . ."

"The polite thing to do would be to go inside and watch a detective show with Mary and Martin."

Eamon groans as he leans against the front of the Land Rover. "It's not the crime-solving priest, is it? That one's the worst. Did I ever tell you that my grandmother wanted me to join the priesthood?"

"I think I'd remember *that*."

"Michael and Patrick both got married straight out of

school, and Keane fled the country the minute he got his Leaving Certificate," Eamon says. "That left me as her last hope. Can you imagine it?"

"I can imagine the seminary bursting into flames the moment you set foot in the door."

He nods. "With the four horsemen of the apocalypse hot on my heels."

"How'd you dodge that bullet?"

"She died."

I burst out laughing, then clamp my hand over my mouth. "Oh my God. I'm so sorry."

Eamon grins. "No need. Gran lived a long and happy life, and her wake was mighty *craic*. In fact, there's reason to believe one of Cathleen's children was conceived that night."

"Cathleen is . . ."

"One of my sisters," he explains. "There are seven of us in total: Michael, Claire, Cathleen, Patrick, Ciara, me, and Keane."

"Do you have a proper saint's name, too?" I ask, recalling something Anna once shared about Keane's real name being Christopher.

"Did my brother tell you about that?"

"Anna did."

"My parents gave their first four children saints' names out of respect for Gran, but after contributing yet another Patrick to a county overrun with them, they decided to give the rest of us usable middle names," Eamon says. "So, Elizabeth is called Ciara and Christopher is Keane."

"And Eamon?"

He scratches the back of his head, one side of his face scrunched up like he doesn't want to tell me—which only makes me more curious. I bat my eyelashes in an exaggerated way, and he sighs. "It's Francis."

"Sexy."

A laugh bubbles out of him. "Fuck off."

I lean in to kiss him. "Come on, Francis, we've got a detective show to watch."

•   •   •

The guest bedroom is an open loft with twin beds and a wooden crucifix hanging on the wall between them. The total lack of privacy seems like a very clear message that nothing sinful will be happening up here tonight. And the crucifix really drives the message home. As if God and the Gallaghers are watching, Eamon gives me a chaste peck on the forehead and climbs into bed. He switches off the volume on his phone and rests it on the nightstand before settling under the covers.

"Good night."

"Night." The sheets are cool as I get into my own bed. It's not very late, so I pick up my phone and send Eamon a text. HEY FRANCIS, WHAT ARE YOU DOING OVER THERE?

His phone vibrates and Eamon huffs as he rolls over to

reach for it, like he's irritated that someone might be texting him at 10 P.M. He reads the message, before laughing softly. "I was trying to sleep."

"Shh." I point to my phone.

He shakes his head as if I'm being ridiculous, but the dimple in his cheek appears as he types out a response. I'M TRYING NOT TO THINK ABOUT HOW FAR AWAY YOU ARE.

My heart does a little dance in my chest because our beds are only a few feet apart. MAYBE YOU SHOULD COME OVER HERE.

> Having sex would be impolite, considering we're guests and strangers. And, if you haven't noticed, there are no walls or doors.

> There are other things we could do together.

> I don't think there are. You're not especially quiet.

A giggle escapes me.

"See," he whispers. "You've just made my point."

> I meant sleeping. Get over here.

The old box springs squeak as Eamon gets out of bed. He creeps slowly, trying to keep the wooden floorboards from creaking, as if Mary might catch him and give him a scolding. I shift on my narrow bed to make room. He stretches out, facing me, and pulls the covers over us.

"This is a terrible idea," he whispers. "I've wanted you all day, and you only made it worse by fixing the Land Rover again."

"You fixed the Land Rover."

He cradles the back of my head, stroking his thumb along my cheek. "Doesn't change the facts."

Eamon is right. We're guests in someone else's home, and it would be incredibly rude—not to mention embarrassing—to leave dirty sex sheets for Mary to wash. But none of that cools the fire of wanting him. The heat radiating from his body surrounds me like an embrace, and there's something about the way he smells . . . it's nothing identifiable, but it gives me the same feeling I get when I'm lying in a hammock under a canopy of stars. Like the whole universe belongs to me. I've never gotten that feeling from another person before.

Why Eamon Sullivan?

Why now?

He leans forward and kisses me the way he did when we were lying in the grass beside the old train station. His hand moves from my head to my back, gently easing me closer, and we lie in the dim light of the bedside lamp, kissing like it's the entire point. Kissing until the questions are erased from my mind. Kissing until the fire he lit inside me is banked to glowing embers.

Finally, Eamon pulls back and drops a kiss on my nose. He switches off the light and reaches for his phone. A few seconds later, mine vibrates with an incoming text.

GOOD NIGHT.

Chapter 10

I'm awakened by the sound of pans rattling on the stove below the loft, and when I open my eyes, Eamon's face is mere inches from mine. His expression is relaxed, and his breath comes out in soft puffs. I watch him, noticing the faint lines at the corners of his eyes and the small brown mole just above his right cheekbone. I'm glad he's still asleep because I'm not ready to acknowledge last night. I'm not good with that kind of intimacy. Sex, sure. But I've had one-night stands that were far less intimate than kissing a fully clothed Eamon Sullivan in a twin bed in a loft in Donegal. It's too much to think about, let alone talk about. Trapped between Eamon and the wall, I close my eyes and pretend to sleep. A few minutes later, he stirs, then gets out of bed. I listen while he dresses quietly and thumps down the wooden stairs.

The questions from last night resurface when he's gone.

I've traveled many places and met plenty of good-looking men, so I can't pinpoint why Eamon is the one who feels at once like the safe cradle of my hammock and the wide expanse of the universe. And it makes no sense that I feel this way after only two days. Except Anna described his generosity when he sailed with her and Keane in the British Virgin Islands. He was raised by the same people in the same environment as Keane, so it's not a surprise that Eamon is every bit as tender and kind. The next question is why would someone like Eamon Sullivan want someone like me? And for that, I have no answer.

I change into a clean shirt and my leggings from yesterday, organize my backpack, make the bed, and join everyone in the kitchen, where Mary has prepared a full Irish breakfast. Our plates are loaded with eggs, bacon, and a variety of sausages, along with baked beans, potatoes, tomatoes, and mushrooms, which Eamon explains is typically Sunday fare. Meaning Mary has gone above and beyond for us yet again.

"It's a long way to Tralee," she offers. "Don't want you going hungry along the way."

"Thank you," Eamon says. "I fear even my own mother's fry-up can't compare."

"Ah, stop it." She waves a hand demurely at him. "It's nothing."

We're stuffed to capacity—at least I am—when Mary brings us a neatly folded stack of clean laundry, and the mud stain on the sleeve of yesterday's shirt is gone. She accepts our hugs of thanks for her generosity. We thank Martin for his help and linger a few extra minutes inside the front door as he offers suggestions about the best route to Tralee. Finally, Eamon says "bye" several times in rapid succession and hustles me outside, explaining as we pack up the Land Rover that Irish leavings often take several goodbyes before the official one. We wave out the window to the Gallaghers as we bump our way down to the main road.

"Such kind people," Eamon remarks, as we follow the road between two pastures, heading in an entirely different direction than the one we'd been following on the railroad trail yesterday.

Just ahead, the bull stands behind one of the stacked stone walls that border the lane. His big head extends beyond the wall, as if he's been waiting there for us.

"Stop," I say.

Eamon pulls the Rover to the side of the lane, and I lean through the open window to take a picture. I reach out and pat the bull between his horns and he doesn't seem to mind. "Later, big boy."

I settle back into my seat and cue up a playlist, leaning against the door to catch the cool breeze on my face. We drive this way for several miles before Eamon says, "Did I do something wrong?"

"What? No."

The words come out too fast and his eyebrows furrow as he gives me a suspicious look, but I'd rather do anything other than talk about my feelings. I don't even enjoy talking to myself about them. I'm experiencing emotions I haven't felt in a long time, but that doesn't change the fact that this is a fling. It comes with an expiration date. And I realize that this whole conversation is happening in my head with Eamon studying me, and ugh . . . feelings are terrible, and no one should have them.

"You've been quiet since we left the Gallaghers," he says. "At the very least I expected a joke about whether the bull looked hungover."

I laugh because I really did miss out on a perfect opportunity. "I'm fine. Just glad to be back on the road."

"You really love it, don't you?"

"It's the only thing I can rely on."

"Meaning?"

"Nothing," I say, realizing I've veered into a direction I didn't want to go. "Traveling is when I'm happiest. That's all."

Eamon lets the conversation lie, but the equilibrium between us is still off. I pick up my phone and pivot on the seat, stretching my legs toward him. When I poke his thigh with my toe, he turns his head to look at me and I snap a photo.

"Is everyone in your family this pretty?"

He laughs. "If you ask Keane, it took our parents six practice attempts to reach perfection."

"Yeah, well, Keane is wrong."

"Get over here, you."

I slide over until I'm beside Eamon. He extends his arm along the back of the seat behind me and presses a quick kiss to my temple. He rests his driving elbow on the open window frame and eventually we slip back onto the same wavelength.

"Did I ever tell you about the time Keane and I rode our bikes to Ballybunion?"

"I just met you three days ago."

"Oh, right." Eamon laughs. "I keep forgetting."

The thing is . . . it does feel like we've always known each other. As if, when he stepped into The Confession Box, we were picking up where we'd left off, rather than meeting for the first time. I can admit that I've never had a fling like this before, but it doesn't mean I want anything more from Eamon. Besides, he's got his own issues. He doesn't need mine added to the mix.

"We were six and seven when we heard there was going to be a surf festival," he says. "Keane was desperate to go, but our parents were too busy to take us, and we didn't have the money for bus fare. If we'd asked, they'd have wanted to know where we were going. And if we'd told them the truth, they would not have allowed two small boys to go to Ballybunion alone. So, we decided to ride our bicycles."

"I assume it was a long ride?"

"It's about thirty minutes by car, but it took us nearly two hours," Eamon says. "We spent the day at the beach, watching the surfers and mucking about in the ocean, and we didn't consider how long it would take us to get back to Tralee."

"Oh no."

He nods. "It was nearly dark when we arrived home. We didn't have mobiles or a way to phone home, and no one knew we'd gone, so the family had organized a search party."

"They must have been terrified."

"Oh, aye, they were," he says. "And they were overjoyed that we were home safe. But after Mom finished her litany of thanks to every saint under the sun, she sent Keane to bed without supper and ate my head off for not being more responsible."

"Is that what you meant the other day when you said you were tired of being the responsible one?"

"She made me my brother's keeper when I wasn't mature enough for the job." His bitterness is unmistakable. "And when her favored son left Ireland, she transferred all her expectations to me. Settle down. Get a steady job. Find a nice girl. Don't be a worrisome lad. Dublin was the end of her leash."

There are things I could say that might make him feel better. I could agree that his mother was unfair and that he hadn't deserved to bear the burden of responsibility for Keane at such a young age. And they would be true. But it's not the truth he needs to hear. "You let her do it."

"What?"

"It sounds like you've made yourself miserable to please her," I say. "I understand that you love and respect your mother, but at some point, it stopped being her fault and became yours."

"Christ," he spits out. "Would you care for a knife so you can finish me off?"

"Look, I don't know your mom, but she adapted to Keane's leaving because she loves him and wants him to be happy. Why wouldn't she want the same for you?"

Eamon's mouth opens and closes as protests begin and end in his brain. Finally, he says, "I never considered that."

"It's probably time to stop resenting your brother for being brave enough to have the life he wants," I say. "And you should talk to your mom about how you want your own life to look, even if it's not what she wants for you."

Eamon falls silent. He remains quiet as the miles pass, but there's no heat in it, no sense that he's angry. He doesn't remove his arm from behind me, and every now and then I feel his fingers against my shoulder, tapping in time with whatever he's working out in his head.

I send Anna a text to let her know we're on our way, and when one playlist ends, I begin another. After nearly an hour of not talking, I apologize to Eamon.

"I shouldn't have said anything. I'm sorry."

He comes back to reality from wherever he's been. "Ah,

no need. You have all the tactfulness of a machete, but you're not wrong."

I laugh. "No one's ever used those exact words before, but . . . that's fair."

"I've been sitting here thinking about everything I'll need to do before I begin my overlanding trip." He glances at me to gauge my reaction and I offer him an encouraging smile. "Obviously, I need to get the coolant reservoir repaired and replace the side mirror. Take a mechanics course. Put the flat up for sale. Quit my job."

Excitement climbs through me when I realize he's serious, and I feel a momentary dip of sadness that I won't be there for any of it. "Life on the road is hot and dirty and sometimes terrifying. Things break and you get lost, but it's worth every minute."

He kisses me quickly. "Thank you."

We spend the next few hours making a list of the equipment he'll need for the trip, and I offer suggestions based on my successes and failures. Time passes so quickly that we're on the outskirts of Ballybunion before I realize that we're nearly to Tralee. Our time together is almost over.

"So, this is the scene of the crime," I say, as we drive into town.

"I can show you around, if you like," Eamon says. "The main road leads down to the cliffs. It's quite spectacular, and since we're nearly to Tralee, there's no harm in a small detour."

"I'd like that."

Except when we reach the intersection where we'd turn onto the main road, there's a cordon blocking the street with a colorful banner that reads BALLYBUNION SURF FESTIVAL. Eamon and I exchange a glance and burst out laughing.

"You've officially come full circle," I say. "We have to go to the festival."

"Anna and Keane are expecting us."

"They've been expecting us since Monday."

"But—"

"You've been dragging your feet around Ireland, and I've gone along with all of it because I get it. *I get you.*" As the words come out of my mouth, I feel as if I've skidded to the very edge of a cliff, loose rocks tumbling into the empty space below. It feels like a declaration, and Eamon blinks. I scramble back to safer emotional footing. "Please . . . do this one thing for me."

He runs his hand up through his hair and I can see he's torn. Behind us, a car honks, reminding us that we're still at the intersection. "Okay."

We park the Land Rover on a side street and join a small crowd milling between the vendor stalls that line Main Street all the way down to the cliffs. There are local restaurants offering a variety of street foods and beers. Artisans selling handmade jewelry, soaps, clothing, and artwork. Surf shops displaying boards, wet suits, and popular brands of surf-related clothes and shoes.

We stop for pints of Guinness and to grab a schedule of events, before meandering hand in hand down the street, weaving around ordinary families enjoying the festive atmosphere and sun-kissed surfers browsing for wet suits and boards. We pause for a moment at a booth featuring sea glass jewelry. I pick up a sterling silver necklace with a teardrop-shaped pendant made from a slice of pale blue polished sea glass. It sparkles in the light, reminding me of the way sunshine reflects off the ocean. The pendant tempts me, even though I rarely wear jewelry.

"You should get it," Eamon says.

"I don't know."

He takes the necklace from my hand and fastens the chain around my neck before taking out his wallet.

"Eamon—"

"It's the least I can do for dragging you all over Ireland," he says, handing some cash to the teenage girl in the booth.

"Thank you."

He kisses my forehead first. Then, my nose. Finally, my lips. "Thank *you*."

We don't linger at any of the other booths as we make our way to the opposite end of the festival. We bypass an empty bandstand with strings of lights delineating a dance floor.

Beyond the bandstand, the road splits. To the left is more Ballybunion, but the right fork slopes down to the beach, where we kick off our shoes, roll up our pants, and walk barefoot to where a small group of spectators is watching the surfers.

The competition isn't until the weekend, but the weather patterns out in the Atlantic have made good waves today. The swells aren't huge, but they're nicely spaced and breaking from the right. There are smaller waves breaking along the beach—the perfect size for beginners—but the best waves are out at the head of one of the cliffs. I close my eyes and imagine paddling out.

"You want to surf, don't you?" Eamon says.

I open my eyes. "Yeah."

"When did you first learn?"

"About five years ago, I rolled into a sleepy little beach village in southern Mexico. I was only looking for a place to camp, but it turned out to be one of the best surf spots in the country," I say. "I ended up staying five weeks and when I left, I had my own board and a full-blown addiction to surfing."

"Keane became obsessed after our Ballybunion adventure," Eamon says. "Sailing, surfing, snorkeling . . . if it had to do with the ocean, he wanted to do it. I enjoyed watching the competition, but it never occurred to me to learn."

"Would you like to learn?"

He takes a sip of beer, considering. "I think I might, but . . ."

But there's no excuse for not showing up in Tralee tonight. Everyone is waiting and we've been selfish long enough. He doesn't say any of that out loud, but I nod in understanding. "I know."

Eamon's phone rings. He digs it from his pocket and glances at the screen. "It's my brother." He presses the button to answer, putting the call on speaker. "Hello?"

"Are you on the way?" Keane asks. "I'm not sure how much longer I can stave off the wolves. My torch is running out of flame."

Eamon and I both laugh.

"We'll be there soon," Eamon says. "We've just made a short stop at the Ballybunion Surf Festival."

"There's a surf festival? Right now?"

"It's pumping," I offer. "Breaking from the right with nice swells at the head."

"Jaysus," Keane swears. "I'll ring you right back."

Eamon and I cross the wide beach to our shoes, and we're ascending the hill toward Main Street when Keane calls again. "We're on our way."

"Seriously?" Eamon says.

"I told Mom I was taking Anna for a wee drive, but we snuck a change of clothes, a tent, and my surf prosthesis out of the house," Keane says. "I reckon if we spend the night, we can go out on dawn patrol and be back to Tralee before the family gathering tomorrow evening."

His rationalizations sound so much like Eamon's the past three days that I clap my hand over my mouth to keep from laughing, but it comes out in a series of snorts instead. Eamon's shoulders shake with his own silent laughter.

"There's a bandstand and some tables at the west end of the main street," he tells Keane. "We'll meet you there."

Chapter 11

"I have several questions regarding your whereabouts for the past three days," Keane says, over a heaping plate of sausage rolls and a round of Guinness. "But first is how the fuck you leave from Dublin and end up in Ballybunion."

He sounds more curious than upset, which is a hopeful sign.

"We legitimately did lose track of time in the pub on Monday," Eamon says, glancing at me for confirmation.

"Understandable," Keane admits.

"But on Tuesday, we did a bit of hiking and camping in the Wicklows. Yesterday we went off-roading in Donegal and ended up spending the afternoon trying to stay out of reach of a sangria-drinking bull," Eamon says. "Today we had no actual plan to stop in Ballybunion, but it's on the way from Donegal, and Carla wanted to go to the festival."

Keane rubs a hand over his scruffy face as he takes in all this new information. "So . . . no last-minute, unavoidable work thing?"

"Sorry, a lie," Eamon says. "Not unlike *I'm taking Anna for a wee drive.*"

She meets my eye as we laugh, but neither of us can get a word in as the brothers volley like they're Federer and Nadal at Wimbledon. I can see she has questions of her own, but I'm not sure I'm ready to answer.

"Fair play," Keane concedes. "You do have the rings, yeah?"

Eamon nods. "They're locked in the Land Rover."

"Land Rover?"

"I bought a Series Three Defender."

Keane's eyebrows climb his forehead. "In the past three days?"

"No," Eamon says. "Two years ago. After I got back from sailing with you and Anna. The plan was to outfit it for overlanding and do some traveling of my own."

Keane blinks several times, like a lens bringing Eamon into sharper focus. "You've owned a Defender for two *years* and this is the first I'm hearing about it? What the fuck, Eamon?"

"I didn't tell anyone," he says. "And then I started seeing Sophie."

"Ugh." Keane rolls his eyes.

"You never met her."

"I only needed one look at her social media. You slagged off on me for *years* about one dull girl I dated for a few minutes when I was twenty-two, then ended up with a dryshite like Sophie."

Eamon cracks up. "That's fair."

"Are you truly planning to go overlanding?" Keane asks, his face and tone more serious.

"I am," Eamon says. "I've got a project at work I need to wrap up and I'll need to do a mechanics course because I'm shite at repairs. I reckon I'll go next summer."

Keane nods repeatedly, the corners of his mouth turning upward until he's full-on smiling. "I'd like to see your Rover."

"Come on, then," Eamon says. "We'll fetch the gear and set up tents on the beach before all the good spots are taken."

"I'll save the table," I say, as they get up. I expect Anna to join them, but she remains seated.

"I'll see it later," she says, as Keane leans down to give her a kiss. I wonder if Eamon would do the same to me if they weren't here. He gives me a sly wink. Yes, he would. I smile.

As soon as they're out of earshot, Anna leans across the table. "What the hell is really happening here?"

"Eamon's going through some things," I say. "I'm just along for the ride."

"Did you sleep with him?"

"In a tent."

She levels a *stop your bullshit* look at me. "You know what I mean."

"And you know me, so you already know the answer," I say. "But I'm not the reason for all his delays. Eamon's trying to reconcile how you can love someone and still resent them. You might not understand how that works, but your sister probably does."

Anna is quiet for a moment, frowning a little, and I know she must be wondering how Ben's death and Keane losing a limb could be considered enviable.

"All I'm saying is that the choices you and Keane made led you to some amazing places . . . and to each other," I continue, realizing I came at her with my machete of truth. "It's kind of hard for the rest of us mortals to see that and not feel inadequate."

"Even you?"

"Nah." I crinkle my nose at her. "I'm living the dream, and if I ever feel like I need someone to love, I'll adopt a cat or something."

"How's your dad?" she asks, and now it's my turn to take the emotional hit, even though I don't think Anna intended the punch to land.

"He's hanging in there," I say. "Stella says there's been a steady decline in his short-term memory lately, though."

"Have you gone to see him yet?"

"No, um—" I take a long drink of Guinness because I don't want to admit that I'm afraid. That I will fall completely apart when Biggie stops remembering me. Except Anna's smart, so she probably already knows. "We've had video chats and I send him pictures from the road."

"Do you think you'll ever go home?"

"I don't know."

"I'm sorry." Anna squeezes my hand. "I shouldn't have brought it up."

"We should have come straight to Tralee."

She waves me off. "Keane's mom is fretting about your delays, but you haven't missed a thing. And it sounds like you've been having some needed adventures."

As we walk to the beer tent for another round, I tell her about the icy stream in the mountains, flipping the Rover, and the finer details of our encounter with the sangria-drinking bull. I don't tell her about how Eamon usually rests his hand on me—my shoulder, my foot, my thigh—when we're driving. Or about dancing in the moonlight. Once upon a time, I'd entertain Anna with my sexual shenanigans, but I keep those moments to myself, too.

"You also had sex with Eamon," she says. "Does this mean you like him?"

"You don't have to like someone to have sex with them."

She shoulder-bumps me. "You're avoiding the question."

"Fine. I like him," I admit. "Otherwise, we probably would have been here a lot sooner, but don't read more into it than that."

Anna shrugs. "Okay, but you could do a lot worse than Eamon Sullivan."

For a moment I allow myself to consider it. To take the fun, warmth, adventure, and toe-curling kisses and extrapolate them into weeks and months and years. But I hit a wall when I think about being Biggie's age, about the possibility of inheriting dementia and putting *anyone* I love through that. It's not something I've ever said out loud to anyone. Not even Anna. So, I brush it all aside with a joke. "I already have."

She laughs. "Well, I'm jealous that you weren't here for the wedding planning. It's not as exciting as you'd think. Especially when *everyone* has an opinion."

I order four more Guinness, then turn my attention back to Anna. "Is your family here?"

"Mom and her boyfriend got here yesterday and—"

"Hold up. Your mom has a boyfriend?"

Anna's mom has been single since Anna and her sister, Rachel, were young, so having someone special in her life is a big step.

"His name is Arno, and she met him at the German-American Society this past winter," Anna says. "She was alone for so long that it's kind of weird for Rachel and me, but he makes Mom so happy."

"Good for her. Go, Ingrid!"

"Rachel, Mason, and Maisie arrived on Tuesday, and Keane's already taught Maisie a bunch of Irish slang words," Anna says, as we carry the beers back to our table. "It's kind of like when she picked up a British accent watching *Peppa Pig,* and I can only imagine her going back to Ohio and calling everyone a feckin' eejit."

"Hey, if they're acting like a feckin' eejit, they deserve to be called out."

She's laughing as Keane and Eamon return, and we spend the next few hours drinking and talking. Although she—and maybe Keane—knows we've slept together, Eamon and I avoid looking at each other too long. And our only point of contact is his knee against mine under the table. As happy as I am to see Anna and Keane, I kind of wish we were still alone.

My phone vibrates in my pocket. I read the message. "Rachel wants to know if I've heard from Anna."

"My mobile is blowing up," Keane says.

Eamon nods. "As is mine."

"It only makes sense," Anna says. "We're all being jerks right now."

"Listen . . . I've held my tongue through a multitude of opinions on our choice of venue, wedding attire, food, music, and the presence of Queenie at the ceremony, not to mention Father Fitzgerald asking us how many children we're planning to have," Keane says. "I believe I've earned the right to be a jerk, especially when the surf conditions are going to be perfect tomorrow."

"So, do we ignore them, or let someone know we're alive?" I ask.

"I'm texting my sister," Anna says, as she thumbs her keyboard. "I told her we needed a break from wedding planning. She suggested we elope."

"How did you answer Father Fitzgerald?" Eamon asks Keane, who grins.

"I told him we already have a dog, but if we decide to have children, we'll be sure to let him know."

With Rachel running interference for us, Keane and Eamon fetch another round of beer. While they're gone, a band starts setting up onstage and the sun sinks below the edge of the cliff. One by one, the vendor stalls close for the night, and everyone migrates to our end of the street. Twilight stretches long at this time of the year, so the light is still fading in the sky as the band begins to play and we find ourselves in the middle of a full-fledged street party.

The band is a traditional Irish outfit with fiddle and penny whistle, and most of their songs are rollicking tunes, but occasionally they slow it down with a ballad.

"Come dance," I say, nudging Eamon's shoulder as I rise. He stands and follows me to the dance floor, leaving Anna and Keane behind.

Eamon takes me into his arms. "I want to kiss you quite badly."

"Anna knows."

"So does Keane."

"Then maybe you should kiss me."

Eamon angles his head down as I tilt my chin up, and our mouths meet in the middle. We drop the pretense of dancing when he takes my face in both hands and skims his tongue along the seam of my lips, easing them apart. I'm vaguely aware that there are people around us, but his mouth tastes like his last swig of Guinness and kissing him never seems to get old. Saying goodbye on Monday is going to be harder than I thought.

He pulls back reluctantly and gives me a slow smile. "Let's get out of here."

"Lead the way."

He takes my hand, and as we pass Anna and Keane on the dance floor, Eamon says, "We'll be down at the tents. Don't feel the need to rush."

Keane winks. "I reckon we'll linger a bit longer."

Eamon and I hurry down the slope to the beach. Stretched out in both directions at the base of the cliffs are clusters of tents. A few have campfires burning in front of them, but so many people are still at the street party that most of the tents are dark. Eamon leads me to his tent. We kick off our shoes and crawl inside, where we kneel face-to-face in the light of a small lantern, kissing hungrily as we shed our clothes.

"Lie back," I say, when both of us are naked.

Eamon stretches out and understanding settles in his eyes as I position myself between his thighs. He licks his lower lip in anticipation. I take his length in my hand and his breath puffs out in a soft *oh*. And when I swirl my tongue around the tip, he nearly levitates off the ground.

I close my mouth fully around him. Eamon slides his fingers through my hair and strokes my cheek with his thumb. I hum with pleasure at the softness of his touch, and he growls in response, his head falling back against the tent floor. As my pace slowly increases, his breath shortens, and his groans lengthen. His fingers tighten in my hair, as if he's fighting against the urge to push deeper into my mouth. I take him deeper.

"Carla." He says my name through gritted teeth. Once. Twice. Each time more urgent than the last. A warning that he's close to the brink that I ignore. "Oh, fuck. Fuck. *Fuck*."

Eamon's hips thrust upward, and with his release comes an inarticulate sound from somewhere deep inside him. I sit back on my heels as he struggles to catch his breath, his hand resting on his stomach.

"I fear my bones have melted into jelly," he says, with a small laugh. "So, if you'd like me to show my appreciation, you're going to need to come sit on my face."

Nothing that I've done to him has been a favor that needs to be returned, but I know what he can do with his tongue, and I'm desperate for it. Eamon grasps me lightly by the hips as I lower myself toward his mouth. The first stroke of his tongue makes my toes curl and draws a moan from my throat. The second sends heat raging through me like wildfire. My head falls back and my hips rock, grinding my most sensitive spot against his tongue. Eamon doesn't try to hold me still or control the motion. He lets me break against him like a wave against a rock, again and again, until my body shudders and I cry out his name.

While I'm lying beside him, he supports his head with one hand and touches my face with the other. "That was the sexiest thing I've ever seen."

I turn my face to kiss his palm. "Thank you for doing it."

He grins. "I can say without hesitation that it was an absolute pleasure."

"We should probably go for a swim," I say. "We're both kind of a mess."

We dig through our packs for swimsuits, and when we emerge from the tent, there's a group of guys sitting around a fire at a nearby campsite. They break into applause, and one of them cries out, "*Oh, Eamon!*"

My face is on fire as we fall apart laughing, and Eamon Sullivan takes a deep bow in their direction.

Chapter 12

Keane's plan to go surfing at dawn is shot in the face when all four of us oversleep after talking around the campfire until late into the night. Anna and I search out a bakery for breakfast and by the time we return, there's already a lineup.

"I've asked around and learned that the surf school has boards and wet suits for rent during the festival," Keane says, over lemon scones and black coffee. "I haven't done much surfing since my accident, so I thought perhaps I could tutor Eamon and Anna while Carla does her own thing."

I nod. "The point break doesn't seem too intense."

"I reckon you know what you're doing," Keane says. "Just respect the locals."

"Of course."

At the surf school, Keane and I help Eamon and Anna

pick out the right-size boards and wet suits. I choose a short board that's closest to the one I own. Leaving the others on the beach—where Keane is giving them a quick lesson—I wade into the ocean and belly onto my board. This is the first I've surfed outside the Americas and I'm excited to catch my first Irish wave.

I paddle to the outside of the lineup, near the cliff head, and sit up on the board to watch the swells roll in. They're a gift from a dying hurricane out in the Atlantic—all the waves, none of the rain—and I'm surprised there's not a bigger crowd out here. Especially during a festival. Until I remember it's a Friday morning and my fellow surfers are probably the die-hards who called off sick from work to be here. I get a couple of nods and one hello, but mostly we're all watching for the right wave. A couple of guys both try for the same big swell, but only one of them gets it.

When I was growing up, no one ever mistook me for the sporty kid. I was never around in the summer to play youth soccer, like nearly everyone my age. And by the time I reached high school, I was so involved in traveling with Biggie that I had no interest in organized sports. Until the year I ended up in Barra de la Cruz.

I was looking for a beach where I could set up camp for the night, but this beach was lively with surfers. It was only later I learned that Barra de la Cruz is one of the best surfing spots in Mexico. I ended up paying next to nothing for a beachfront site in a tiny, rustic campground populated by tents, camper vans, and one other Jeep.

I'd just finished rigging my hammock when an Italian guy came by to tell me he'd made dinner for everyone in the campground. We sat in plastic chairs around plastic tables until the early hours of the morning, eating carbonara, drinking beer, and cobbling all our languages together so we could understand one another.

The next day, I walked along the beach to the headlands, where the surf was most intense. As I watched the surfers, I could almost imagine the Zen-like feeling of cruising along the bottom of a wave. My stomach muscles shifted as the surfers made powerful cutbacks. I felt the rush of adrenaline as they did aerial tricks. Surfing was not something I'd ever done with Biggie. It was something new, something just for me, and I wanted it. I watched until I felt the sun burn my nose, then walked to the surf school and signed up for lessons.

Five years later, on a beach in western Ireland, I watch my wave roll in. I'm still not an expert, but I'm not afraid to catch it. I turn the board and paddle until I feel the lift. Pop up. Steady myself. Immediately fall over. Come up laughing. Do it all over again.

After I've ridden several waves, I notice Anna, Keane, and Eamon have joined the lineup. I sit on my board and watch as Anna picks up a wave closer to the beach and rides it all the way to shore. And I watch Eamon wipe out. He pops up, spluttering and grinning, and I paddle over to him. "Having a good time?"

"I can't say I've been bitten by the bug." He kisses me with cold, salty lips. "But I'm glad I learned, and I'd probably do it again, in the right company."

"That's fair," I say. "I thought I'd hang out with you for a while."

"Aw, did you miss me?"

I laugh. "I don't miss anyone when I'm surfing. But if I'm going to stand up for Anna tomorrow, I don't want to be in pain while I do it."

We spend a couple more hours surfing, goofing around, and making videos of our wipeouts. Afterward, we return the equipment, grab a late lunch at the festival, and pack up our gear. The family gathering at the Sullivan family pub starts in just under two hours, but Eamon assures me we'll have plenty of time to shower and change before the festivities begin.

"Since Mom is already upset that you're late to Tralee, we'll go on ahead," Keane says, as we stop first at their rental car. "I'll shoulder the responsibility and calm her down."

Eamon fist-bumps his brother. "I reckon she's upset with you now, as well, but thank you."

"Yes, well . . . it's the least I can do. We'll see you at home."

"Can I ask what that was about?" I say, as we walk to the Land Rover. "Feel free to tell me it's none of my business."

Eamon waves me off. "Yesterday, Keane and I talked about . . . a lot of things. I confessed that I've been feeling a bit resentful of his life, and he pointed out, rightfully so, that my resentment is not his fault. I also mentioned that part of the resentment stems from having always been the one to bear the blame when we got into trouble together."

"What did he say about that?"

"I thought perhaps he'd try to play innocent, like he was unaware it was happening," Eamon says. "But he admitted he's always known and apologized."

"Ah, okay, so he gets to take the blame for today."

"We're still on the hook for the rest of the week, though," Eamon says, with a small laugh. "Keane and I have never been at odds over any of this—it's all played out in my head—but the air between us is properly clear."

"Glad to hear it. Are you ready to go home now?"

"Truth be told, I'd rather spend more time alone with you," he says, pressing me gently against the Land Rover. He kisses me again and again, until he pulls away reluctantly. "I'm sorry for dragging you into my mess."

"I have no regrets."

"You'll also be pleased—and not at all surprised—to learn that Keane supports my scheme to quit my job and drive around the world," Eamon says, as we load our gear into the Rover.

"Maybe he can help soften things with your mom."

He nods. "Maybe."

We pass beyond the border of Ballybunion a few minutes later. The coastline recedes, replaced by broad swaths of farmland. Eamon no longer needs the GPS, but as he turns off the regional road to a narrower local road, I wonder if he's still delaying the inevitable.

Before I can ask, I notice a large brown-and-white hawklike bird perched on a fence, holding a wriggling gray animal in its talons. I'm about to make a joke about natural selection when my mind processes that its prey is a *kitten,* and suddenly fuck natural selection.

"Stop!" I cry, and Eamon mashes the brakes so hard the Land Rover skids and the tires spit gravel.

I fling open the door and jump out, startling the bird. It lifts off from the fence with huge sweeping flaps into the blue sky overhead. I hurdle the fence and give chase, waving my arms and shouting, hoping the bird will release its prey. It's about fifteen or twenty feet in the air when the kitten wrenches itself free and plummets to the ground.

I keep my eye on the bird for a moment, hoping it won't circle back for another shot, but it flies away. I rush to the general area where I think the kitten landed, then slow my pace, careful with my steps, until I find the animal. The kitten is a shade of gray that's almost blue and looks like velvet, and while I'm no expert on cats, it seems barely old enough to be separated from its mother.

I pick up the kitten as gently as possible and turn it over to find a small puncture in the middle of its chest, the gray fur around the wound stained with blood. Without X-rays, it's impossible to tell if the kitten sustained any injuries in the fall, but when it mewls, it doesn't sound distressed. The puncture wound can't feel good, but the kitten seems to understand that I'm not here to cause it further harm.

"We can't leave it," Eamon says, as I return to the Land Rover with the kitten in my arms. "Even if it has no other injuries, it will still be at risk from another hawk or a fox. And finding out where it came from might take hours. My sister is a vet at our local SPCA. She can patch it up and find it a home."

"Guess it's your lucky day, little guy," I say, as Eamon unearths a first aid kit from under the passenger seat, grabs a bottle of water from the cooler, and rummages through his duffel for a bar of soap.

I restrain the kitten as best I can while Eamon dabs at the wound with a cotton ball soaked in sterile saline. His touch is gentle and his voice soft as he tells the kitten that everything will be okay.

"It doesn't appear to be a very deep wound," he says. "You interrupted the hawk before it had a chance to do any lasting damage."

Eamon covers the wound with a soft cloth bandage before wrapping it with gauze. Our towels are wet and sandy from surfing, so I offer a clean wool T-shirt from my backpack, which he uses to form a nest in the middle front seat. He carefully deposits the kitten in the nest, fluffing up the sides to make it cozier and more secure. The gesture is so sweet I can barely stand it.

Taking Eamon's chin in my hand, I give him a tiny squeeze and a smooch. "You know, this is how Anna and Keane ended up with Queenie."

He laughs and rolls his eyes as he swings up into the driver's seat. "I have plans now. And they don't include cats."

"I'm just saying."

"I'm not keeping it," he says, picking up his phone. "But I'll ask Cathleen to bring some cat food to the pub. It's probably hungry."

I tickle the kitten behind its tiny ears. "You are never going to make it to the shelter."

Eamon scoffs. "Please. I can resist."

"Tell me another one, St. Francis."

He laughs as he shoves the gearshift into first. "Feck off."

Biggie and I had the occasional goldfish, but never any actual warm-blooded pets. We spent the entire school year in Fort Lauderdale, but in the summer, Biggie didn't think we had enough room in the Jeep for a dog or cat. And later, when I was on my own, it didn't seem fair for me to keep a pet when I was working double shifts to earn travel money. I've met plenty of people on the road who travel with their animals, but never really considered trying it myself. "Do you know how to tell if it's male or female?"

Eamon shakes his head. "Cathleen will know."

"Your reaction time when I shouted for you to stop was extraordinary."

"You sounded panicked," he says. "Although I haven't known you long, panic seems wildly out of character for someone who came face-to-face with a bull and didn't flinch."

"I couldn't let that hawk eat this poor baby."

Eamon's cheek dimples. "You know what I think?"

"What?"

"You want the kitten."

"Shut up," I say, but as we drive in silence for a few long moments, the green countryside rolling past my window, I realize that it's not a terrible idea. I've been traveling alone for so long that it might be nice to have some company. "Do you think it would require a lot of red tape to bring it to Florida with me?"

If Eamon made fun of me right now, he'd be justified. I'd sit here and take it because I was the one who dished it out in the first place. But he doesn't even snicker. "I don't know, but we can find out. I'm sure vaccination records are involved, but my sister can see to those."

"Thank you."

"For what?"

"For stopping," I say. "And for not teasing me when I deserved it."

His smile is warm. "You launched yourself out of the Rover, ready to do battle with a hawk. And this kitten wasn't going down without a fight, either. The way I see it, the two of you are made for each other. That said, I reserve the right to make fun of you at another time, when you're not expecting it."

I laugh. "Totally fair."

The houses start getting closer together and the farmlands fall away. We pass the Tralee welcome sign, and it isn't long before we reach the center of town. Eamon parks in the first empty spot he finds. Because of the kitten, we've lost the time we needed for showers and a change of clothes. They'll have to take us as we are.

The family pub is not far up the road on the opposite side. The two upper stories of the building are painted a pale shade of teal with window boxes bursting with red, yellow, and white flowers. The street level is darker teal with SULLIVAN'S PUB painted in gold across the wide front window.

"Ready?" Eamon asks, reaching for the handle of the teal front door. There's a sign affixed that reads CLOSED FOR PRIVATE PARTY.

"The question is, are you?"

He laces his fingers through mine. "I am now."

Chapter 13

We step into the pub and the first thing I notice is that everyone is nicely dressed in pants and button-up shirts, skirts, and dresses. Even Anna and Keane had time to shower and change into clothes more appropriate for a family dinner. The pub goes utterly still as the entire Sullivan and Beck families turn to look at us. We must be a sight, with our hair stiff and messy from salt water, and our flip-flops dusted with sand. My shorts are a little damp from pulling them on over wet bikini bottoms, and Eamon's still wearing swim trunks patterned with yellow pineapples. On top of everything, I'm holding a kitten wrapped in a T-shirt.

Eamon offers a tentative "hello" and the room explodes into a barrage of questions. *Where have you been? What took you so long? What were you doing? Why didn't you phone? What the devil were you thinking? How could you be so irresponsible?*

They come at us so fast that I'm not sure who's doing the asking, but the last question—the bombshell—comes from a petite older woman I can only guess is Mrs. Sullivan. Her dark brown hair is shot through with gray strands, and she wears round tortoiseshell glasses that magnify the disappointment in her eyes. Eamon visibly sags beside me, and I give his hand an encouraging squeeze. Her gaze falls on our linked hands. Eamon lets go.

"Ah, this must be the kitten you mentioned." A younger version of Eamon's mother steps forward carrying a medical kit. She's somewhere in her forties with Sullivan-brown hair and hazel eyes like Keane. This must be Cathleen.

Her question defuses all the others, and she carefully scoops the T-shirt nest from the crook of my arm. The kitten wakes up with a tiny mewling yawn.

"Look at this wee darling," Cathleen says. "Where did you find it?"

Eamon embarks on a detailed account of how I rescued the kitten from a hawk, and as he holds everyone's rapt attention, I remember how he told me he was a natural actor. From behind the rest of the family, near the end of the bar, Keane raises his Guinness in a toast. By the time Eamon has completed the story, all the children—including the teens—are gathered around Cathleen while she examines the kitten. Even Mrs. Sullivan is momentarily enchanted by the tiny gray ball of fluff.

With everyone distracted, another Sullivan sister approaches. She's younger than Cathleen. Closer in age to Keane and Eamon. Since he mentioned that Claire is the eldest sister, I assume this is Ciara.

"If you want a wash before dinner, now's your chance," she says quietly to Eamon, but offers me a conspiratorial smile. "But be quick about it. We can't hold her off much longer."

We snatch our packs off the floor and slip out through the back of the pub. I follow Eamon up a flight of wooden stairs to the apartment on the second floor. It's small and cozy with lots of framed snapshots of Ciara posing with a good-looking blond guy.

Sand trickles out of my bikini into the bottom of the bathtub as I strip off my clothes.

"I think we should shower together," Eamon suggests.

"Dude, we don't have time for sex right now."

He laughs. "As much as I appreciate that your mind went directly there, I only mean to save time. Even I'm not foolish enough to delay this party any longer than we already have. You saw my mother's expression."

"I don't know why I'm afraid of someone who looks so tiny and sweet."

He laughs. "Welcome to my entire existence."

We bathe quickly and dress even faster. Eamon tucks a pale gold shirt into a pair of navy chinos as I swipe gloss across my lips, hoping the wrinkles in my yellow floral sundress look deliberate instead of messy. Less than ten minutes later, we reenter the pub, looking as if we've planned our outfits. Which I'm certain will only raise more questions.

In our absence, Eamon's sisters have taken control of the party. The men are carrying platters of food from the kitchen under Ciara's direction, while Cathleen marshals the kids around their own table, all while bottle-feeding the kitten.

"She doesn't appear to have sustained any major damage," she says, handing both the kitten and the bottle to me. "But I'd like to bring her to the clinic tomorrow morning before the wedding for X-rays, just to be certain. She's on the cusp of being weaned, so I've brought some replacement milk as well as wet food."

Eamon plants a kiss on her cheek. "You're grand. Thank you."

"It was nothing." She gives him an affectionate swat. "You're still in quite deep with Mom, so behave for a bit, will you?"

He grins. "I'll try."

Several tables have been pushed together so that all the adults and their partners are sitting at one long table with the elder Sullivans at each end, far enough away that Eamon's mom and her anger can't reach us. Mr. Sullivan's hair is pure white, but his face is youthful, and he has the same mischievous smile as his youngest son.

My seat is between Ingrid Beck and Anna, with Ciara directly across from me, beside the blond guy from the photos in her apartment. He's even more good-looking in real life, but his eyes are glassy, as if he's already had too much to drink.

"Who's your new friend?" Anna asks, as I sit.

"We just found out she's a girl," I say, looking down at the tiny creature in my arms. Of all the unexpected things that have happened over the past several days, adopting a kitten is the most surprising. It's only been a few hours, but I can already feel the strings attaching. I don't know what I'll do if she can't go back to Florida with me. "So, I'm not sure what her name is yet."

Eamon leans around Keane to look at me. "She's a fighter, that one. We should—I mean, *you* should consider calling her Maeve, after the warrior queen."

Keane nods in agreement. "A very good suggestion, although calling her Rosie may help land you back in Mom's good graces."

"How upset is she?"

"More confused than angry," Keane says. "You've always been the sensible lad with the college education, steady income, and girlfriends who are minus *craic,* so it comes as a bit of a shock to her system when you show you're actually a right fucking mess."

"Sorry, can we back up a second?" I say. "What's minus *craic?*"

"The opposite of *craic,*" Ciara interjects. "Hanging around the graveyard would be livelier than Eamon's ex-girlfriends."

As the rest of us howl with laughter, Eamon looks like he might want to argue that point. Until, finally, he shrugs a single shoulder. "I thought if I dated women who had their lives in order that orderliness might rub off on me. Instead, they all dumped me because . . . I'm a right fucking mess."

He laughs a little to himself. "Sophie expected a ring. I bought a Defender."

"The better investment, if you ask me," Keane says.

"And the *craic*'s been ninety," Eamon says, as his eyes meet mine. We share a private smile.

Until Keane clears his throat, reminding us that we're in public. My face flares with heat. At one end of the table, Mr. Sullivan clinks his pint glass until everyone has quieted down.

"Now that we're all finally here," he says, leveling a look at Eamon, "I'm thankful to have everyone together under one roof for such a joyous occasion. If you'll please join hands and bow your heads, we'll give proper thanks before the food gets any colder."

The family recites what I think is the Lord's Prayer and afterward, as the food and conversation flow, Eamon's transgressions are forgotten—at least for now. Ingrid Beck introduces me to her new boyfriend, Arno Schneider. And I spy an engagement ring on Rachel's finger as she introduces me to Mason. Anna identifies everyone else at the table.

"Michael is a police sergeant, and his wife is Claudine," she says. "Claire is an interior decorator married to Neil. You've met Cathleen. Her husband is Brian. Patrick is a divorced dad who runs his own construction company. And Ciara's fiancé is Dominic."

"A few more beers and I won't remember any of this," I say.

She links her arm through mine. "I'm glad you're here."

"Thanks for putting up with my shit."

"And thank you for putting up with mine," she says, resting her chin on my shoulder. "Now, what's really going on with Eamon?"

"Nothing," I say, quietly. "I told you yesterday, it's just a vacation fling."

"I saw the hand squeeze at the door."

"Do I have to be in love with him to offer moral support?"

Anna cocks her head. "Okay, but the two of you have an obvious connection. Have you considered maybe this isn't just a fling?"

"You heard him yourself. He's a hot mess."

"Maybe he needs someone who knows how that feels."

I nearly choke on my Guinness. "God, Anna, I'd hate to hear your opinion if you weren't my best friend."

She laughs and kisses my cheek. "I love you and I want you to be happy."

"Yeah, I know," I say, as she turns to listen to something Keane is whispering in her ear. And softer, to myself, I add, "Me, too."

As evening stretches into night, the empty plates and food

platters are cleared away, and the drinks begin flowing faster. We push away from the tables and talk in clusters that swell and ebb as people come in and out of conversations. I meet all the people Anna pointed out during dinner and eventually find myself face-to-face with Eamon's mother.

Like her husband, she's aged gracefully, and I can see Eamon's smile in hers, just before she registers me and the smile slips from her face.

"Hi, Mrs. Sullivan," I say. "I'm Carla, Anna's maid of honor."

"I know who you are," she says, a touch of iciness in her tone. "But what I'm trying to work out is what role you played in Eamon's late arrival."

She cuts straight to the chase, and I pause to remind myself that diplomacy is my friend. "Well, the detours were his idea, but I didn't talk him out of them. Respectfully, this is a conversation you should probably be having with him."

She squares her shoulders. "Oh, I fully intend to—"

"He doesn't need a lecture," I say, cutting her off. "He needs you to listen."

There's a steeliness in the delicate arch of her brows and I realize immediately that I've gone too far. "I shouldn't have said that. I'm sorry. It's just that Eamon loves and respects you . . . maybe to a fault."

"There's no fault in respecting your parents," she says, dryly.

"Of course not." I soften my tone. "But Eamon works so hard to please you that he's made himself miserable."

Her defensive stance deflates. "He told you that?"

"Not in so many words," I say. "But he has dreams he's kept to himself because—" I stop myself. "He needs to be the one to tell you this. Please, just try to listen."

She places her hands to her cheeks and sighs. Behind her glasses, her eyes are shiny with unshed tears. "I had no idea."

"He keeps a lot inside," I say. "I'm certain this is not how he intended for this to go down. Also, I'm sorry for, well . . . he says I have the tactfulness of a machete."

"You do cut to the heart of it."

I laugh. "It's a gift and a curse."

"Thank you." Mrs. Sullivan reaches out and gives my arm a gentle squeeze. "Pardon my manners. I do believe we've gotten off on the wrong foot. It's lovely to meet you, Carla. Welcome."

"It's lovely to meet you, too."

She takes a deep, shaky breath. "I reckon I need to find my son."

I smile. "You've got this."

As she walks away, I double-time it to the bar, where Keane is pouring himself a glass of cider.

"I'd take one of those, if you don't mind."

"That looked a bit intense," he says, sliding the full glass across the bar, then beginning a second pour.

"Little bit."

He snorts a small laugh. "On the bright side, you made it out alive."

"Listen, I've spent most of my adult life dealing with cranky old people in Fort Lauderdale," I say. "She doesn't scare me."

Keane laughs harder. "Sure about that?"

"Okay, I lied. She's terrifying."

"Now you understand why I always let Eamon take the fall," he says, then falls silent and reflective for a short time. "Yesterday, when he shared his resentments and the dreams he's kept secret, I couldn't understand why he hadn't trusted me with them. He's always been my best mate. There was nothing better as a child than having a built-in playmate and Eamon always went along with my schemes."

I take a sip of cider, wondering where Keane is going with this.

"Anna pointed out that Eamon has always been swept up in someone else's plans. My childhood mischief. Our mother's ideals. His ex-girlfriends' aspirations. Even Gran wanted him to be a priest. Can you imagine?"

Remembering my conversation with Eamon about this, I bite back a smile. "I mean, in a dirty sort of way."

Keane forms a cross with his index fingers and extends it at me. "Get behind me, Satan. I don't need that in my head."

We both laugh, but he turns serious again. "At first, I reckoned that Eamon shared everything with you because you have no skin in the game. Your feelings won't be hurt, and you're leaving on Monday."

I nod. "Sometimes it's easier to talk to a stranger than it is to your best friend."

"Except, you're not a random stranger, are you?" Keane says. "You've lived the life Eamon's only dreamed about, so you were the perfect stranger. You didn't unlock the door, but you sure as fuck handed him the key."

"Is that . . . good?"

He laughs. "It's very good. It's what he's needed."

"Will your mom agree?"

"The thing is, she's stubborn but not inflexible. It simply takes a bit of time for her to bend her mind," Keane says. "I was not quite six years old when I knew I wanted to see everywhere there is to see, so I spent my youth preparing her. She didn't like it when I left, but she accepted it. She'll come around."

"I'm happy to hear that," I say. "Eamon is . . . well, he deserves . . . he should be happy."

"Feel free to tell me to fuck off, but I think you make him happy," Keane says, with a wink. "And having you in my family wouldn't be the worst."

"Ugh," I say, smiling at the idea of me, being a part of this family. Being a part of Eamon's life. Even though it's not going to happen, it's a nice idea. "Fuck off."

• • •

"Do you want a lift to the hotel?" Ciara asks, as I stand in the doorway of the bar. Nearly everyone has left. The chairs are all overturned on top of the tables and Dominic is mopping the floor.

"Isn't that out of your way when you live upstairs?"

She rolls her eyes at me. "Do you want a lift or not?"

I glance back. Eamon and his mother are perched on the only barstools still on the floor, facing each other, deep in conversation. Their heads are nearly touching, and her hand is resting on the back of his neck. They've been that way for the better part of an hour. I don't want to disturb him to let him know I'm leaving, so I hitch my backpack up higher on my shoulder and tuck a drowsy kitten a little closer to my chest.

"Okay," I say. "Let's go."

Ciara's car is a little red Volkswagen Golf, and she zips through the streets of Tralee like she stole it. "Anna tells me you're a barmaid back in Fort Lauderdale."

"I am. How about you?"

"Same," Ciara says. "I've been managing the pub for the last year and a half. Since Da had a heart attack and his doctor told him he needed to find a new hobby."

I think about how bartending has always been a means to an end for me. Maybe in a different life I'd have chosen something else, but it puts cash in my pocket the fastest way I know how. "Do you enjoy it?"

"Not at all," she says. "But I don't have the heart to tell my father he should sell the bar when it's woven into the fabric of our family."

"Oof, yeah. I can understand not wanting to do that," I say. "What would you rather be doing?"

"Before I came back to Tralee, I was an archivist at the National Museum of Ireland in Dublin," she says. "I'm not too high and mighty to be pouring beers for the punters, and my relationship with Dominic is short-distance now instead of long. But I really miss my work."

"You gave up that job to run a bar?"

Ciara shrugs. "What else could I do? My older siblings have families and Keane was on the other side of the world. It should have been Eamon, because you can do computers remotely these days, but Mom wouldn't hear of it. Eamon's her favorite."

I bark out a laugh. "He told me that was Keane."

"Keane is the baby, so he gets away with murder," she says. "But no, the sun rises and sets on Eamon. She's always come down hard on him so he wouldn't turn out like Keane."

"God, your family is messy."

"What family isn't?"

I look out the window and think about Biggie, about our own family mess. I've been running for so long, afraid to face the day when he doesn't remember me. But what if my dad dies and I spend the rest of my life regretting that I wasn't there? I've trusted him all my life, but what if he was wrong? I'm caught off guard when a tear trickles down my cheek.

"Doing okay?" Ciara asks, as I wipe my face with my fingers.

"Exhausted," I say, trying to laugh away the torrent gathering behind my eyes. "Today has been a wild ride."

She stops the car in front of a building that resembles a Regency manor. I half-expect a footman to come forward and open the car door for me. When no one appears, I open the door and step out, adjusting my backpack and the kitten once more.

"A long soak in the bath and a good night's rest should set you to rights," Ciara says. "I'll see you tomorrow at the wedding."

"Thank you for bringing me."

She gives me the classic Sullivan grin, a dimple forming in her cheek. "Thank you for saving me from having to close down the pub."

I stop at the front desk long enough to pick up my room key. As soon as the door closes behind me, for the first time in years, I break down and cry.

Chapter 14

The kitten—I'm still not sure about calling her Maeve—is sleeping in her nest when I settle against the headboard and FaceTime my dad. Biggie still has his own cell phone, but Stella usually answers first so she can prepare him for the conversation.

"Hi, hon!" she says, brightly. If she notices my swollen eyes or red nose, she has the grace not to mention it. "How's the Emerald Isle?"

In the background, I can hear Peter Fonda asking Jack Nicholson if he's got a helmet. It's a line I've heard dozens of times. Biggie must be watching *Easy Rider* again.

"It's been an adventure," I say.

"Biggie, it's Carla." Stella turns her head away briefly as she speaks to him, then looks back at me. Her voice is quieter as she says, "If there's any blessing at all in this infernal disease, it's that he frequently gets to see his favorite movie for the first time."

The TV goes silent. A few seconds later, my dad's face appears on the screen.

"There's my favorite girl in the whole world." When he smiles, my chest constricts, and fresh tears sting my eyes.

I've staved off homesickness for years, always moving, always distracting myself with new places, new faces, new experiences. But here, alone in this room on the edge of Ireland, I can't push the feelings away. There's nowhere for them to go.

"Hi, Biggie," I say, relieved that he seems to know who I am. "How's it going?"

"Oh, you know. Same shit, different day, but I'm losing my memory, so it seems like new shit every day."

I try to laugh, but it comes out as a snotty sob.

"Hey," Biggie says, his voice soft. "What's going on? Why the tears?"

"I miss you."

"I miss you, too," he says, but I can't help wondering if he still knows how to miss someone. "Tell me all about Ireland."

Even though I recognize the tactic as his way of distracting me, I tell him about camping in the Wicklows. He roars with laughter as I tell him about our encounter with the bull in Donegal. I talk about the surf festival in Ballybunion, and how I rescued the kitten from the hawk. I pan my phone over the sleeping kitten. "So, I guess I have a cat now."

"She's precious," Stella says. "It'll be good for you to have some company on your next adventure."

"I, um—I've been thinking about coming home."

Neither of them speaks for what feels like an eternity. I know Stella is staying out of father-daughter business, but I'm having trouble interpreting Biggie's silence. Will he be mad at me? Or will he welcome me home?

His bristly brows furrow and his eyes narrow with anger. "It's too late for that, Sheryl. We're all happier here without you."

"Biggie, honey," Stella says, gently. "That's *Carla*, remember? She's your daughter."

"Aw, fuck." He buries his face in his hands. "I'm sorry."

"It's okay, Dad. I know you weren't talking to me."

He disappears from the screen and Stella's expression is sad. "He's a little agitated, so I'd better go."

"I'll talk to you later," I say. My voice cracks. "Love you both."

I disconnect the call. It was good to talk to Biggie, but I don't feel any better. I don't know how my chest can ache and feel scooped out at the same time. I want those lost years back. I want my dad back.

I've wasted so much fucking time.

The gentle white glow of the clock on the bedside table tells me it's not as late as it seems. I didn't drink enough to get wasted or eat enough to be stuffed, so I roll onto my side and pull the duvet up to my ears. I lie in the dark as the minutes turn into an hour, simmering in a stew of regret and sadness.

The door opens with a gentle click and a strip of white light illuminates the wall as a dark, Eamon-shaped form comes into the room.

"How'd you get in?" I ask, switching on the light.

"The hotel receptionist was preparing to leave for the night as I came in," he says, unbuttoning his shirt. "I patted down my pockets and pretended as if I'd misplaced my room key. I told her my wife probably had it in the room."

I prop my head on my hand, watching as he removes the shirt, letting him distract me. His hands fall to the button on his pants.

"She studied me for a moment, then said, 'Eamon Sullivan, is that you?' And it turns out it's Aisling McCarthy, a girl I knew from school," he says. "I considered telling her she'd mistaken me for someone else, but she went on to say, 'I saw your ma while I was getting the messages at SuperValu, and she never mentioned you'd gotten married.'"

I snort a laugh. "Busted."

Eamon's pants drop to the floor, and he steps out of them. "So, I said, 'You've caught me in a lie, Aisling. I'm here to fetch my brother's fiancée. You see, we're desperately in love and we're planning to run away together.'"

My mouth falls open. "You did *not*."

"Oh, but I did," he says. "And after she was properly

scandalized, she traded me the key for the sheer thrill of possessing what she believed to be the hottest gossip in decades."

"You're definitely going to hell for that," I say, as he eases his boxers down past his hips.

Eamon's cheek dimples. "Among many other things."

When he's completely naked, he sinks to his knees and lifts the bottom end of the duvet, exposing my feet. He cups my heel and presses his lips to the side of my foot, just below my ankle.

"It looks like you had a good talk with your mom," I say, as he feathers soft kisses up the inside of my lower leg, toward my knee. He moves onto the bed, still beneath the duvet.

"Later," he murmurs against my skin. "Busy right now."

His lips trace an achingly soft path up my inner thigh, his pace unrushed, deliberate, as he moves my underwear aside. Memories of our first night together still fresh in my mind, I squirm with anticipation. He slides his tongue against me in a long, slow stroke that draws a low moan from my throat. My hips arch as Eamon repeats the movement. I want him to devour me. I want him inside me. Instead, I surrender to the exquisite torture of his tongue until he leaves me shuddering, my hands clenched around fistfuls of sheets.

My breathing is uneven as Eamon's lips graze a spot just below my navel. I want to say something to break the quiet intensity, but he moves again, kissing his way up my stomach, his body moving over mine. He kisses me between my breasts, then on my chin, my nose, my forehead, and finally my mouth. Eamon lowers himself to the mattress beside me, kissing me the way he did at the train station and again in the Gallaghers' loft. As if he didn't just make me melt. As if I can't feel his erection pressing against my thigh.

"Why do you do that?" I ask.

"What?"

"Just . . . *kiss*."

His eyebrows dip in confusion. "Because kissing for its own sake is fun. Have you never—"

"No."

Sex has only ever been about the good time, about escaping things I didn't want to acknowledge, even with Camilo. When your brain is fogged by lust, you don't have to examine your feelings. There's no shame in emotionally disconnected sex, but I don't enjoy the feeling that maybe I've been missing out on something . . . more. Or that I'm having this revelation right now.

My brain and body are usually in agreement on what sex means, but Eamon's tenderness has thrown me out of sync. Without another word, I swing a leg over him and straddle his hips, trying to lead him to a different place. He drags his lower lip between his teeth, distracted as I rock against him, and the conversation is over. Except, when my panties are off and the condom is on, Eamon pulls me gently forward until our chests are touching. He cradles me there as our bodies move together in a slow and steady rhythm, kissing me again and again and again.

Afterward, I snatch up my underwear and hurry to the bathroom under the guise of washing up, so Eamon won't see the fresh tears in my eyes. I sit on the bathroom floor with my back against the locked door, heels of my hands pressed to my eyelids, until he knocks.

"Everything okay?"

There's no answer I can give him that will make sense. The last thing I need right now is to be in love with Eamon Sullivan. I don't want to be in love with him. But as the past four days replay in my head, I think . . . maybe . . . I am.

Fuck.

I splash cold water on my face before opening the door.

"I'm fine," I say, moving past him before he can put his hands on me. Before he can kiss me. "It's just been a long day, and I need some space."

"Huh," he says, as I climb into bed. "Okay." I can feel him looking at me a little longer, but eventually he leaves to wash up.

I pretend to be asleep when he returns, but as soon as the warmth of his body is beside mine, I feel the pull. Like he is the moon and I'm the tide. Loving and hating the feeling in equal measure, I turn to face him. "I'm sorry if I seemed snappy earlier. Today's been a lot. How did things go with your mom?"

"After admitting that she's not thrilled with the idea of me giving up a secure job to take to the open road, she said I need to do what I need to do," he says. "Which is likely the closest I'll ever get to her blessing."

I search his eyes because I can't get a sense of how he feels. "And?"

"She apologized for not giving Keane his share of the blame," Eamon says. "I've never had that kind of conversation with my mother. Ever. Having her regard me as an adult has done my head in a bit, but it was good. It was really good."

I smile. "What are you going to do now?"

"Keane suggested I let the flat instead of selling, which is a sound idea," Eamon says. "And I'll keep working as long as possible to make sure I don't run out of money during my travels."

"Sounds like you've got it all figured out."

"You, um—you could come with me."

The unsettled feeling from earlier returns. "Why are you asking me this now?"

"I . . . don't know." There's a hesitation in his voice that wasn't there a moment ago. "These past few days have been the most fun I've had in a long time, and—"

I get that edge-of-a-cliff feeling again. I could jump and hope that Eamon will catch me. Or I can step back. "That's how vacation flings work."

His eyes meet mine. "Is it a fling, though?"

"What else would it be?"

Eamon doesn't immediately respond, but I hear the answer all the same. He clears his throat. "Something more."

"I warned you not to do that," I say, as the corners of his mouth turn down. "I'm leaving Ireland in three days and I'm already taking one stray home with me."

"Jaysus." Eamon sits up. "You can pretend you don't feel it, but I know you do. Why are you like this?"

"I don't know, Eamon. Maybe it's because my mom left me behind and it's only a matter of time before my dad forgets I exist," I spit back. "I learned a long time ago that the only person I can count on is me."

He blinks. "What? What do you mean about your dad?" The understanding mixed with confusion on his face only makes me feel worse.

"Because this"—I gesture between us—"is not meant to be something more. I don't owe you my life story."

"Fine," he says. "But it's still utter shite. Anna has never abandoned you and you love her."

"That's because she would never ask what you're asking."

"I didn't fucking ask you to marry me," Eamon says. "I thought we were having a good time together and that you might want to continue it a little longer. If you've had enough of me, you didn't need to start a fight. You only needed to tell me to leave."

We stare at each other; my eyes flick away first.

"Maybe you should go."

He flings back the covers and gets out of bed. Without trying to argue his case, he gets dressed. He doesn't look at me. Doesn't speak to me. He doesn't even slam the door behind him.

"This is why you never sleep with the best man," I tell the kitten when he's gone, but even I don't buy into my bullshit. I rejected Eamon because I'm scared of getting close. Scared of losing him before I even have him. Because I was trained at the knee of the master.

Chapter 15

I oversleep. After a fast breakfast and faster shower, I hurry to Anna's room to get ready, thanking the wedding gods that I cut off all my hair. Rachel is already decked out in the flowy, pale green chiffon bridesmaid's dress that Anna picked out for us. Ingrid is tucking bits of baby's breath into Anna's loosely braided bun. Anna's ivory dress is lacy and backless, making her look like a beautiful fairy queen.

I tell her so, as I kiss her cheek. "Keane better watch out or I might steal you away."

"Oh my God." She laughs out loud. "There's a rumor going around the hotel that Eamon and I were planning to elope together. How in the world did they get that idea?"

I feel an uncomfortable pang when I think about how last night ended, but I paste on a smile and shrug. "What? That's ridiculous."

Once I'm zipped into my dress, I let Rachel mess with my hair and apply my makeup. She lends me a pair of sparkly earrings and Ingrid unearths a pair of lace-up leather sandals from her suitcase. I feel another pang as I remember Biggie's tenet about traveling light. None of these things would have fit in my backpack and my dress would have been a wrinkled mess. I had to rely on the kindness of others to bring them to Ireland because I've been incapable of bending my father's arbitrary rules. My breath catches in my chest as I realize that Eamon and I are exactly alike, keeping our feelings bottled up. Following the rules that other people made for us. It's no wonder we pull toward each other like magnets.

As Rachel and Ingrid do some last-minute fussing over Anna's hair—making me realize I'm utterly useless as a maid of honor and possibly as a friend—I walk over to the window and look out. Wooden folding chairs have been set up in rows on the wide beach, facing the ocean, and a wedding arch draped with pale green and ivory bunting and bits of greenery.

Keane and Eamon are already out there, dressed similarly in tan pants, crisp white shirts, and leather shoes, with Queenie parked at Keane's feet. He's wearing a tweed vest to identify him as the groom, and the effort he's made to tame his wild hair is touching, if not wholly effective. My eyes come to rest on Eamon, who looks as handsome as ever, and his words echo in my ears. *Why are you like this?*

"Carla." Anna slips her arm through mine, bringing me back to the room. "Ready?"

"Absolutely," I say, with a smile. "Let's go get you married."

•   •   •

When I was a little girl, my dad kept a photo of his wedding to my mom in his wallet. Maybe he still has it. I haven't seen the inside of his wallet in a long time. The photo was a grainy and slightly out of focus image of my giant hippie dad in an ill-fitting suit standing beside his too-young bride outside the clerk of courts building. I loved it so much that sometimes I'd ask to borrow a dollar, just to get a peek at it. I memorized my mother's smile and the way her long black hair cascaded over her shoulder. Biggie never made me pay back the money I "borrowed" but he also never explained why she left or asked me how I felt about it.

All this time I thought I'd adjusted to a life without a mother, but as I watch Anna walk down the aisle with Ingrid and Rachel, I feel like a person-shaped empty space. Like my whole life has been me, faking at being human. I'm mad about so many things. That my mom left. That Biggie taught me the art of distraction instead of letting me mourn her loss. That despite everything, he's still my favorite person and the thought of losing him makes me want to set the world on fire. That someday I might become my father and lose everyone I've ever loved. And I'm mad that Eamon Sullivan was somehow the person who unlocked this Pandora's box that I can't seem to shut.

I glance at Eamon on the other side of the wedding arch and he's watching me, his brows lowered with concern, and I'm angry that he can *see* me. I smile, laugh, and clap in all the appropriate places, and when I cry, my tears aren't just for Anna and Keane. But all I can think about is going home to see my dad. About figuring out which parts of my life have been real, and which have been pretend.

· · ·

The vows have been witnessed, the cake served, the toasts made when I knot my dress around my knees and walk down to the beach. The tide is low and the air smells briny as I stand in ankle-deep water and look out at the horizon. Home is not directly across the ocean, but it's my next destination. It's time. This is how Eamon finds me, his own feet bare and his pants rolled up to his calves.

"Hi," he says quietly, standing beside me.

"Hi."

"I'm sorry for making you uncomfortable last night."

My heart aches with fresh pain that he would apologize for something that wasn't his fault. "Eamon, you did nothing wrong. I owe you an apology for lashing out over something that has nothing to do with you."

"Would you care to talk about it?"

"No, but also . . . maybe?"

Even his laughter is kind as he takes my hand. "What's troubling you?"

"My dad has dementia," I tell him, as we walk along the shore. "It's not new. He was diagnosed several years ago, but . . . Biggie was my whole world when I was a kid. He was dad *and* mom. Teacher. Best friend. Traveling companion. You said at The Confession Box that it sounded like my childhood was idyllic—and in so many ways it was—but he also taught me how to sidestep messy emotions."

"Get in a Jeep and drive away."

I nod. "Get in a Jeep and drive away."

"That's what you meant about your dad forgetting you exist."

"When he was diagnosed, I was going to move back home to help manage his care," I explain. "But Biggie didn't want his dementia to ruin my life, so he made me promise I'd keep traveling. I loved him and idolized him, so I kept the promise. But now, his condition is worsening, and if he dies while I'm in some far-flung corner of the world, I'll have to live with that regret forever."

Eamon squeezes my hand. "With context, last night makes more sense, and my offer still stands."

I snort a tiny laugh. "As much as I appreciate your willingness to travel with an emotionally stunted woman, I *have* to say no. I have to go home. I can't be away anymore, I won't."

"I could wait—"

"Please don't do that," I say. "I need to focus on Biggie, and you . . . you've just taken your first steps into a wider world. You need to keep going."

"It won't be the same without you."

"No," I say, swallowing down the parts of me that want to run away with him. "But it will be a good different. You'll have exciting adventures and meet so many interesting people along the way, and maybe one of them will be The One."

His eyes are glassy as he shakes his head. "I'm afraid I've already met her, and now I have to let her go."

"The other thing I didn't tell you"—I pull in a shaky breath—"is that there's a chance what's happening to Biggie might also happen to me. I can't do that to someone else."

"There's also a chance that it won't happen."

"Eamon—"

He takes my face in his hands and kisses me the same way he did in the elevator the first night we met. Like a promise that this is just the beginning. Except, trying to start a long-distance relationship after knowing each other six days wouldn't be enough—or fair. I don't know whether to laugh or cry, so I do both. He gathers me in his arms, and I bury my face against his neck.

"God, Eamon, how are you still single?" I say, with a watery laugh, repeating the question I asked when we first met. "Seriously, how?"

"Because never once have I ever met anyone who makes me feel the way you do, immediately and wholly," he says. "You make me happy. You make me wild. And I don't think I'll ever get you out of my system."

"I'm sorry things can't go a different way," I say. "But mostly I'm sorry that the one time I meet someone I might love, it's the wrong time in my life."

Eamon pulls his head back. "Did you just tell me you love me?"

"No, I said I *might*."

A slow grin lifts the corner of his mouth. "You love me."

"Don't get your hopes up, Francis."

Eamon's mouth stretches beyond dimples into something far too joyful for what basically amounts to a breakup. There is no long-distance option when one of us will be traveling the world and the other one will be settling down. No putting our lives on hold until we're both on the same page. No scenario that turns this fling into the "something more" it wants to be. And yet Eamon Sullivan is smiling. "You *love* me."

"I don't know why you're so happy about this," I say. "I'm leaving."

"Because I knew we both felt it."

I shake my head. "You're ridiculous."

"Perhaps. But you love me."

"Fuck off," I say, as he reels me in for another kiss. "You can't fall in love with someone you've only known for a few days, but if that were possible, then yes, I love you."

He kisses my nose. "I love you, too."

Chapter 16

"You're leaving already?" Anna says over breakfast the next morning, when I tell her Eamon and I are heading back to Dublin. Her family is planning to stay an extra week to do some sightseeing around Ireland. That was my original plan, too, but the longing to go home has grown from an itch into a full-blown need. "I thought you were going to take some time and explore."

"I kinda already did that." I start out with a joke—my usual way—but after telling Eamon about my dad's condition, I'm starting to realize that I've shared my adventures and ridiculous antics with Anna but left out many of the most important things. I continue more seriously. "You and Keane will be busy getting the boat ready to make another transatlantic crossing and, well . . . I miss my dad."

Her eyes widen, but I notice the tiny upward shift at the corner of her mouth. "You're going home?"

I nod. "I've asked Stella if I can have my old room back, and I'm sure she's already hauled all my old stuff out of storage."

"Wow. That's a big step for you. How are you feeling about it?"

I take a deep breath and let it out slowly. I don't really know what my life, or my relationship with my dad, is going to look like. "Scared. I hate that I'll be there when Biggie permanently forgets me, but I'd never forgive myself if he died while I was away. Or for letting Stella handle it all alone."

"I wish I had something wise to say." Anna reaches across the table and squeezes my hand. "If you need me, say the word and I'll drop everything to be there."

I blink to hold back the tears. I've cried more in the past few days than I have in my entire life, and I'm kind of over it. "If our friendship has ever felt one-sided, I'm sorry if I dropped my end."

Anna holds up her hand to stop me, shaking her head. "Carla, I got on a boat and sailed away without telling anyone, but I never once panicked about our friendship because I knew you'd understand. I know you'll be there when it counts."

"I've been pretty unreliable this week."

She makes a *pfft* sound. "This was not my circus, not my monkeys. If I'd had my way, Keane and I would have been married on a tropical island with only Queenie as a witness. Or, honestly, we probably wouldn't have gotten married at all."

"Really?" I'm a little shocked by the revelation. If any two people were made to be married, it's Anna and Keane.

"Keane's devotion to his mother is . . ." Anna trails off and I laugh, understanding all too well from my time with Eamon.

"What I wouldn't give to have that kind of power," I say.

She laughs. "Right? Anyway, you, standing beside me when I got married, is all that I needed. Which takes me back to my original point. Our friendship has always meant having each other's backs when it matters, so if you need me, you only have to ask."

"Thank you." I squeeze her hand in return. "I will."

Eamon comes down from my hotel room carrying both our bags over a single shoulder. Things are a little awkward between us, but not in the way I'd initially feared. We've reached a mutual understanding that when I get on the plane tomorrow, our relationship is over. The weirdness comes from neither of us wanting it to end or having a solution that will make it work.

Keane is hot on his heels, and when we're all together, we say our goodbyes. Hugs and kisses. Promises to be safe. A bit of small talk about the likelihood of traffic. And finally, the rapid series of "byes" signifying that it's really time to go.

The Land Rover sits on the circular driveway just outside the front door, looking slightly more battered than the first time I saw it. I wonder what it will look like after Eamon's had his adventures and how strong the bond between man and machine will be. It seems silly to have a connection to a vehicle, but I wouldn't trade my Jeep for anything.

From the hotel, we drive to the SPCA, where we meet Cathleen. She x-rayed the kitten before the wedding and boarded it at the clinic while we were all busy with festivities.

"No internal injuries or broken bones," Cathleen says, handing me a small carrier with the kitten inside. "She's fully vaccinated, and I've signed off on all the paperwork you'll need to import her to the States. Since you're a US citizen returning home with your pet, I doubt you'll have any issues."

"Thank you for everything."

"Have you decided on a name?"

"Maeve," Eamon says, at the same time I say, "I'm on the fence about Maeve."

He blinks. "Why? It's a good name."

"It's very Irish."

Eamon gives an incredulous laugh. "She's an Irish cat that you found in Ireland."

"I know," I say. "But I'm not Irish, so I was thinking about calling her Boudica, after the English warrior queen."

Cathleen pinches her lips together to keep from laughing as Eamon's eyebrows shoot up toward his hairline.

"There have been plenty of women warriors through the ages," I continue. "Hatshepsut, Cleopatra, Deborah . . . and that's only ancient history. There's Lagertha, Xochitl, Joan of Arc—"

"But English?"

"She existed during the Roman Empire," I protest. "There wasn't any England or Ireland, just a bunch of Celtic tribes."

Eamon gives me a wry grin, and I realize he's been messing with me the whole time. "Boudica is also a good name. Not that you need my blessing."

• • •

Without detours and delays, the route from Tralee to Dublin is a straight shot across the country, and we arrive at Eamon's apartment in a little more than three hours. He drops me off at the building and we unload our camping supplies onto the sidewalk before he gives me the key to his apartment. While he's parking the Land Rover, I move everything into the lobby and take Boudica upstairs and put her carrier on the balcony where she can have some fresh air. By the time I return to the lobby, Eamon is there to help carry everything else.

After the last load, he catches me in his arms. "Is there nothing I can do to convince you to stay a bit longer?"

With no job and no travel plans, I could stay a few more days, but leaving tomorrow is going to be difficult enough. Better to make a clean break.

"I'm sorry. I need to go."

His lips find the side of my neck and my resolve weakens. "Are you sure?"

"I'm positive, but feel free to continue your persuasions, if you like."

Eamon's response is the wicked laugh I like so well, and he leads me to his bedroom, where our clothes end up in a heap on the floor. The first time we are ravenous for each other; the second time feels like goodbye.

"What are your plans when you get home?" Eamon asks, tracing lazy circles on my shoulder as we lie tangled together in his bed.

"I'm not sure the bar where I normally work has the payroll to hire me back right now," I say. "But I'll find something and spend my free time with Biggie."

"Will you miss traveling?"

"I don't know. My dad kind of programmed me for this life, so I don't really have a sense of who I am without it."

"I think you give him too much credit," Eamon says, cradling my cheek in his palm. "Sure, he may have fostered your sense of wanderlust, but . . . look, I haven't known you long, but it's clear you're not the type of person to continue doing something that makes you unhappy. You know who you are."

I turn my face and kiss his palm. "What are you going to do next?"

"I've been thinking it might be possible to work remotely,

so I've arranged a meeting with my boss," he says. "He may not agree to it, and it'll likely lead to a demotion, but . . ."

"You can work *and* travel," I say, finishing his sentence. Leave it to Eamon to figure out how not to fly by the seat of his pants. I respect him so much for that. "A very smart, very Eamon Sullivan thing to do."

"It's not considered cheating in the overland world?"

"The reason I never made it to Tierra del Fuego is because I ran out of money. My Jeep was running on fumes, and I had *maybe* twenty dollars left when I limped back to Fort Lauderdale," I say. "It's not cheating to have a safety net."

"Hey," he says, kissing my forehead. "Completely different subject, but I was wondering if you could help me with something."

"Sure."

Eamon gets out of bed and pulls on a pair of sweatpants. I yank on a T-shirt and shorts and follow him into the hall, where he opens the storage closet with all his camping gear. He removes several unassembled cardboard boxes, which he takes to the living room.

"I think it's time for Sophie's shite to go."

We pack up the throw pillows from the couch, the geometric art prints hanging on the wall, various tchotchkes, the plants in the fireplace, and a row of beige books she'd selected for the aesthetic rather than the subject matter. When we're finished, he steps onto the balcony and snaps off a single bloom of jasmine, which he tucks into the slit at the top of one of the boxes. Then, he calls Sophie on speaker.

"It's Eamon," he says.

"Hello," she says, warily. "How was the wedding?"

"Grand. Listen, I'm phoning to let you know that your things are in the lobby. Just buzz and I'll let you into the building to collect them."

"I've got a meeting tomorrow, but I may be free on Tues—"

"I'm afraid today's the only day that will work for me," he says. "If you can't make it, you'll find them in the bin tomorrow. Can't guarantee they'll still be there by Tuesday."

"But—"

"Sorry, no time to chat. Bye." He disconnects the call and looks at me, his eyes wide. As if he's shocked himself.

I golf clap, my voice just above a whisper. "Masterfully done."

He laughs, his head swiveling as he looks around the apartment. "The place looks empty."

"For now," I say. "But just think of all the cool things you'll collect on your travels. Someday this place will say *Eamon Sullivan lives here,* and the woman who appreciates that will be The One."

Eamon takes me in his arms and holds me for a time that

feels both long and entirely too short. "I hate that she won't be you."

"Yeah. Me, too."

• • •

Eamon refuses to drop me off at Arrivals, a gesture that would make Biggie Black proud. Instead, Eamon parks the Rover and walks with me to the ticket counter. I'm carrying Boudica in the small carrier from Cathleen, while he pulls the suitcase that he gave me when I realized my backpack was too small to fit everything I'm taking home. I broke Biggie's rule because sometimes you do need to carry a bigger load—and I'm realizing that following arbitrary rules isn't always the best way to go through life. Sometimes you need to make your own rules.

Once my bag is checked, he stays with me until we reach the security queue. Eamon kisses me softly. Slowly. Then presses his lips to my forehead. "If not me, let Anna know that you've made it home safely. She'll tell me."

I slip my arms around his waist, breathing in his scent, memorizing the feel of his body against mine, one last time.

"I will."

"And if your circumstances ever change, promise you'll call me."

"Only if you promise that you understand that sometimes people come into your life when you need them and then leave forever," I say. "Promise that you won't wait around for me."

There's a resolute firmness in the gesture when Eamon shakes his head. "I'm never going to agree to that."

"How are you still single?" I ask, for the third time since we've met, making him smile.

"Because you're not mine yet."

"Eamon—"

"Listen," he says, taking a step backward. "I've got a meeting and you've got a flight, so I'm going to leave before I make this goodbye even more difficult."

I close the gap, kissing him hard. "I love you."

He grins. "I know."

I give him the finger, and the last thing I see before I'm swallowed up by the security queue is Eamon Sullivan laughing.

Chapter 17

My rideshare pulls into the driveway of the house where I grew up, in the historic Sailboat Bend neighborhood of Fort Lauderdale. Dad used nearly all his savings on a down payment after my mom fell in love with a little lime green cottage with a white picket fence and a gumbo limbo tree in the front yard—or at least she fell in love with the *idea* of all that. The clapboards are painted a sunny yellow these days and there's a porch swing hanging from a branch of the tree, where Stella likes to sit on cool evenings with a romance novel and a glass of Moscato. There used to be a tire swing in that spot with a patch of dirt beneath it where my feet wore the grass away. Before I became a wench in a pirate bar, and Stella replaced the patchy grass with sod. But none of the changes she's made have ever stopped this house from feeling like home.

I thank the driver as I get out of the car and snap a quick

photo before Stella comes bursting out the front door, waving like I've come home from the war. She stands on the porch steps wearing white capri jeans with a red polka-dot halter top.

"How's he doing?" I ask, as she envelops me in a hug and a cloud of Charlie perfume that tickles my nose. It's been her signature scent since the seventies. She really is perfect for Biggie. "How are *you* doing?"

"Oh, I'm fine. And your dad has his ups and downs." She links her arm through mine as we step through the front doorway into the house. "Tell me all about Ireland and the wedding. I didn't see any pictures on your Instagram."

"I haven't had time to sort through them yet," I say, which feels every bit as disingenuous as it is. I've never curated my posts. I don't overthink social media. I upload immediately unless I don't have an internet connection. But even when Eamon is not physically present in my Ireland photos, I can't separate him from the experience. The subtle arch of Stella's eyebrows says she doesn't believe me.

"Ireland is gorgeous and every bit as ridiculously green as you think it is," I say, scrolling rapidly past most of my pictures until I find one from the wedding that Mason took for me during the ceremony. "Anna and Keane got married on the beach so their dog could be part of the celebration, which is completely on-brand for them."

A dull ache swims through my chest as I think about the last night Eamon and I spent together, after we finished kicking Sophie's memory to the curb. I don't think about the sex. Instead, I think about how, when I closed my eyes that night, I knew that when I opened them in the morning, I'd find him beside me. How he makes . . . how he *made* me feel so much less alone in the world. I wouldn't be here if he hadn't been there.

"And I brought someone home with me," I say, opening the travel carrier and telling Stella the story of how I saved Boudica from the hawk.

"Sweetie, I want to hear every last detail of your trip, but would you mind sitting with your dad for a bit?" Stella asks. "I need to get out of the house before I smother him with a pillow."

I blink, slightly alarmed. "What?"

"I'm sorry. I don't mean that." Her shoulders sag and she fans her face to keep the tears at bay. "Sometimes I get angry with him for being so helpless, even though it's not his fault. A respite caregiver comes twice a week so I can run errands or go to Zumba, but occasionally I have the urge to get in my car and drive to a hotel in Key West where I can just be alone."

"Well, I'm not going anywhere, so now's your chance."

"I'll be fine." She blows out a breath. "I needed to vent a little, and maybe I'll go get my nails done. That always makes me feel better."

"I came home to help," I say, giving her hand a quick squeeze. "I know Biggie didn't want me to see him deteriorate, and I wanted to honor his wishes. But while I was in Ireland, I realized that I need to be here with him, even if it's hard."

Stella smiles softly as she reaches up to tuck a strand of hair behind my ear. "I wondered how long it would take you to figure that out."

"You could have said something," I sputter.

She giggles and rolls her eyes. "You're as bullheaded as your father. You had to reach the conclusion in your own time."

"Go to Key West. I've got this."

Stella gives me a tight hug, then her wedge heels thump on the hardwood floor as she goes off to pack. I drop my suitcase inside the door of my old bedroom. The walls used to be purple and covered with mementos of school friends, travel friends, photos, and posters of pop punk bands I would never admit to liking today. Now the room is crisp white with framed photos of Biggie and me in various locations around the world. The bedspread is purple, which makes me smile, and there's a plastic tote marked CARLA'S STUFF on the floor under the window.

I cross the hall to Dad's room. I'm afraid to open the door, not knowing what to expect when he's living on borrowed time. When I haven't been here to know what to expect. I'm relieved to find him napping on his own bed on top of the covers. His black-rimmed glasses are folded on the nightstand, and he's wearing his favorite heathered maroon sweatshirt and matching sweatpants. The first time he ever wore them, I told him he looked like a Honey Baked Ham, and beer spewed out of his nose as he laughed.

Smiling at the memory, I plop down on the chair in the corner of the room. Stella's humming drifts down the hall as I share my Ireland photos with the internet. I start with the selfie outside The Confession Box. I try not to let my brain get stalled out by doubt as I post pictures of Eamon, but when I reach the photo of me, lying in the heather, I hesitate because anyone who's paying attention will be able to see the exact moment that I fell in love with him. A lump fills my throat.

I skip over the photo, and by the time I'm finished sharing the rest, Stella's suitcase is loaded in the trunk of her yellow VW Beetle that has eyelashes on the headlights. She hands me a glittery pink binder filled with detailed information about taking care of Dad and shows me where she keeps his medications.

"Don't forget that he can't drink anymore," she says. "I know how you two liked to listen to music and have a few beers, but alcohol interferes with his meds and makes him confused."

"Maybe we'll go get tattoos instead."

She laughs. "Don't you dare."

Back in the bedroom, I watch from the doorway while she turns on a gentle alarm to wake Dad gradually.

"Whenever he's startled out of sleep and disoriented," she

explains, softly, "he has a harder time than usual remembering people."

His eyes flutter open. He reaches for his glasses and as he sits up, he offers Stella an uncertain, yet delighted grin. I wonder how many times he's fallen in love with her.

"Hello, Biggie." Her red lips curve into a bright smile. "Feeling better?"

He nods, getting to his feet. "I am. Thanks, Stella."

"Hiya, Honey Baked," I say from the doorway.

Dad turns at the sound of my voice and breaks into laughter. "There's my girl. How was . . ." He taps his knuckle repeatedly against his forehead, then blows out a frustrated breath when he fails to remember where I've been.

"Ireland," I remind him, as he catches me up in a monster hug. He smells the same and his arms feel just as safe as they always did. "Before the wedding I went camping in the Wicklow Mountains and did a little off-roading in a Series Three."

His puzzled expression lands like a punch to my heart. I quickly find a picture of Eamon's Land Rover, but the light in Dad's eyes doesn't shine as bright as it once did when it comes to cars. He doesn't seem to recognize the vehicle or remember that he always wanted to restore an old Defender. His smile is genuine, though. "Wowee! That's a fine-looking machine. I wouldn't mind having one of those."

"I know, right? It was so cool."

"Listen, Biggie," Stella says. "I'm going to Key West for

a couple of days, but Carla is going to stay here with you. Is that okay?"

"Can't think of anything I'd like better."

He leans down to kiss her—not unlike a bear kissing a bunny—and she swipes a smear of red lipstick off his mouth with her thumb. "I love you."

Dad crinkles his nose at her. "Love you, Stella Bella."

There are tears in her eyes as she leans toward me for an air kiss. "If you have any problems, call me and I'll come straight home."

We walk together to the front porch, where Dad and I watch Stella back down the driveway, a plastic flower dancing on her dashboard.

"I gotta tell you, kid," he says, as we go back inside. "I can't always remember her name, and sometimes I can't place her at all, but every time I look at her, I feel like I must be the luckiest guy in the world."

I nudge him with my elbow. "Just so you know, she was thinking about murdering you earlier."

He laughs, but his smile fades quickly. "Taking care of me has become a full-time job. I can't drive or go for a walk by myself because I get lost. I need to look at the house numbers to remember my address. This morning, I made myself a bowl of cereal for breakfast and put the milk away in the cabinet under the sink. Sometimes I'm aware of how frustrating I am and I can't stop myself, but most of the time I don't even know when I'm being a pain in the ass."

Biggie sent me away so I wouldn't have to deal with his dementia, so now I don't know how to deal, what to say, or what to do. "Do, um—do you want to watch a movie?"

"Nah."

"Listen to music?"

"Yeah, okay."

We sit in the living room—Boudica on my lap—sipping sweet tea and listening to Joni Mitchell's *Blue* album spilling from the speakers of Dad's old turntable. He closes his eyes. I wonder if the album is a new experience for him every time he listens, or if she's carved into the deepest grooves of his brain. Either way, I don't want to spoil the magic by asking.

As we listen, I send my memory as far back as I can go, to the day I started first grade. I was already an independent kid, but Dad still parked the Jeep and held my hand as he walked me to my classroom. My T-shirt had a hand-painted portrait of Stevie Nicks on the front that Ugly Louie had made for my first day of school, and I was confused when the teacher asked me if Biggie was my grandpa. I remember him coming to pick me up from a fourth-grade sleepover in the middle of the night because I had a nightmare. He had my back when I got in a fight in seventh grade after another girl shoved me against the wall. Biggie stepped into the principal's office, where we were both waiting for our parents, and I was scared that he would be angry or disappointed.

"I don't condone violence, and Carla knows she's not allowed to start a fight with anyone for any reason," he told the principal. "But if someone picks a fight with my daughter, she has my explicit permission to finish it."

I still got the mandatory three days' suspension—and he did not win any goodwill points with the administration—but in every action, Biggie made it clear that he would never abandon me. Even now that dementia has him in its grip, he's still trying to be the man I remember, even if he doesn't always remember himself.

When that final piano note of the last song fades away, Dad opens his eyes and they're shining with unshed tears. Joni Mitchell is still in there somewhere, but he doesn't repeat his beloved story about how the first thing he did after he returned from Vietnam was hitchhike to Berkeley to see her play.

"We've argued so often about music," I tell him. "But never about Joni."

The corner of his mouth hitches up uncertainly, and I wonder how many times my heart can break. "Never about Joni."

Dad takes a black three-ring binder from the coffee table and hands it to me. It's thick with pages, and when I open it, I discover that it's part scrapbook, part autobiography, with photos and notes about everything from his childhood home in Ocoee to his life with Stella and me. There are pictures of me at every stage of my life, including a few that Stella must have downloaded and printed from my Instagram account. I feel a surge of guilt that she had to do that when I could have come to see him in person.

"Stella made it to help me remember. It doesn't always work, but it's a good story that I enjoy reading." He clears his throat. "My favorite parts are always about you."

"My favorite parts are always about you, too, Dad."

He taps a sticky note on the cover of the binder. On the note is a list: *Ireland, Anna's wedding, Jeep, music, work.*

"She also gives me . . ."

My mouth wants to rush in and provide the missing words—conversation starters or maybe topics of interest—but I wait, letting him finish on his own.

"Stuff to talk about." He sighs, and I understand those weren't the words he was looking for. I wonder if Stella feels this constant ache in her chest and I wonder if it was a good idea to come home. I could call her back. I could get in my Jeep and drive away. Pretend I never even came here.

"Ireland was beautiful," I offer, starting with the first suggestion on Stella's list. "And while I was there, I fell in love."

"You did?"

Biggie and I have never talked about my relationships, mostly because they don't last and usually aren't worth discussing. But what happened with Eamon was different. And eventually Dad will forget everything I say, so it seems safe to tell him.

"He slow dances to 'Harvest Moon,' loves Tolkien, owns the entire Discworld series, helped me rescue Boudica from a hawk, and gives the best forehead kisses." My voice cracks and a tear trickles down my cheek. Fuck. I'm not supposed to miss Eamon. And I sure as hell was not supposed to love him. "He is smart and kind and way too good for me."

Biggie reaches out and wipes the tear away with his thumb. "You don't believe that, do you?"

"Just trying to make myself feel better about cutting him loose."

"Is that working for you?"

"Not this time."

He's quiet for a few beats. "I know I used to have the answers, and I hate that I don't anymore."

"Yeah," I say, sadly. "Me, too."

Chapter 18

Dad is still asleep when I go to his room the following morning, equipped with Stella's down-to-the-minute schedule of his day. It's written on paper, but also programmed into his smart watch so he doesn't have to rely on memory. Every morning he does laps in the pool with a notification to start and stop, so he doesn't have to count. His breakfast is prepared and waiting in the fridge for warming up. She lays out his clothes, so he doesn't have to decide what to wear. But there's an underscored note on the schedule that says: IF HE WANTS SOMETHING DIFFERENT THAT'S NOT AN UNREASONABLE REQUEST, LET HIM MAKE THAT DECISION.

Biggie's alarm clock plays the gentle melody, gradually increasing in volume until he wakes. He seems disoriented as he sits up. He puts on his glasses, and when he looks at me, his eyes widen. "Sheryl?"

Mom has been gone for nearly thirty years. We've never tried to track her down—at least not to my knowledge—and she's never been in contact with us. No birthday cards. No Christmas gifts. If she's been following my progress, she's given no indication. But today, she's here, if only in Dad's mind.

I clear my throat and channel my mother. "Hi, Biggie."

"What are you doing here?"

"I was in town," I say. "Thought I'd swing by and see how you're doing."

"Well, it's good to see you." He swings his bare legs over the edge of the bed. "A little weird that you're in my bedroom, especially when I need to get dressed, but, uh—stick around, okay?"

"Okay." I step out into the living room, where I consider the ethical implications of pretending to be my own mother. Maybe it will help Dad gain closure. Does he know he needs closure? It's more likely he won't remember the conversation. Either way, it feels weird, but he clearly doesn't realize I'm not Sheryl.

Dad comes out of the bedroom wearing black jeans and a Pink Floyd *Dark Side of the Moon* T-shirt that's older than me. The prism is faded and crackled, and the fabric has turned a soft black. If he weren't such a damn giant, I could make a fortune selling his vintage band shirts to teenage girls.

"Can't believe you still wear that shirt, Big."

He laughs as he smooths his hands down the front. "Just got it broken in the way I like it." He sits in his leather recliner. "What brings you to Lauderdale?"

"Class reunion." As the words leave my mouth it feels like I've gone directly for his jugular, but he doesn't seem to make the mental connection. "How's Carla?"

He pauses, and for a moment I think he might be back. His eyes flicker down to the sticky note from Stella, uncertainty written across his face. "I think she might be in Ireland for Anna's wedding, but maybe she's at work. My memory isn't what it used to be."

I sit down on the couch, not far from his chair. "Sorry to hear that."

"Yeah. Me, too." He gives a small chuckle. "I had a lot of good memories."

We fall silent for several long moments. There are so many things I could make my mom say. I could manufacture a whole life for her that was too big and busy for a husband and daughter. She could apologize for leaving him. "You, um—you did a great job raising her, Biggie. You should be proud of yourself."

He huffs, leaning forward in his chair. "I used travel as a distraction because I didn't know how to be a father to a five-year-old, Sheryl. I kept her occupied, kept her moving so she wouldn't have time to miss you. Sometimes I think I did Carla a disservice . . . I spent so much time shielding her from her emotions that now she has trouble connecting with others in a meaningful way. And when she does, she just gets scared and runs away."

The tears come too fast for me to hold back. His memories may be fading, but his assessment of me is so razor sharp that the pain steals my breath.

"Hell," he continues, "I pushed her away with my 'here for a good time, not for a long time' bullshit because I wanted to spare her from watching her old man become a babbling, incoherent mess. Face it, Sheryl, we've both been shitty parents."

"Wanting to protect your daughter from pain is the opposite of shitty, Big."

"I should have been better."

I take a deep breath. Let it out slowly. Look him in the eye. "You were always there when I needed you. And that's what counts."

He's quiet for a few beats, then blinks. I can almost see his awareness coming back online. His eyes grow shiny with tears. "You have always been the best part of my life, Carla, and I hope you can forgive me."

I get up from the couch, kneel in front of my dad's chair, and give him a hug. "There is absolutely nothing to forgive, Dad. Just let me come home."

• • •

As we walk out to Valentina, I think about how Biggie planned the Jeep with me in mind. The desert gets scorching, and riding around with the top down can be hard on your hair and skin. Instead of getting a soft top, he chose the model with a hard top and air-conditioning so I would always be comfortable. The Jeep came with a soft top too, but it's sitting unused in a storage unit, and changing it this late in the game would feel sacrilegious.

As I make a little nest for Boudica between my electric cooler and the driver's seat, I realize I may have to do some reconfiguring of my own.

"Buckle up," I say, as Biggie climbs in. It's been a long time since I've seen him on the passenger side. He adjusts the seat as far back as it will go and pulls the seat belt across his chest.

"Remind me where we're going?"

"Picayune Strand."

Biggie's brows furrow, like he's working hard to find that memory. "Have I been there?"

Picayune is a national forest made up of cypress swamp, pine flatwoods, and wet prairies. It's where the "sell you some swampland in Florida" figure of speech originated, back when some shady developers sold tracts of unusable wetlands to gullible buyers. And it was one of the first places Dad took me off-roading after he bought Valentina. Since Florida is mostly flat with sandy soil, the state is not known for rock crawling and mountain trails, but rainy season in the Everglades makes for great mudding. We drove down trails flooded with water deeper than the tires, and through gullies that splattered the Jeep so thick with mud, it completely concealed the paint.

"Yeah," I tell him. "We went camping there one summer and the mosquitos nearly carried us away."

Biggie laughs. "That I can believe."

"Do you remember why you came back here after Vietnam, instead of settling somewhere else?" I ask.

"I may have been the black sheep of my family, but Florida has always felt like home to me," he says. "I appreciate how the environment does its best to shake off human life like a tick. How we essentially live outside, even when the doors are closed and the windows shut."

I laugh because he's right. Critters are always trying to get inside, and if you drop your guard for too long, your whole backyard will be overtaken by an army of wild plants, screaming, *We were here first!*

"My secret reason for coming back," Biggie continues, "was because I always hoped that maybe another Florida kid who was raised like me might see that patterns can be broken."

"You've never told me that before," I say.

"I've kept it to myself," he says. "But apparently secrets don't mean much to my new reality."

I smile, even though his new reality is sobering. "Why Fort Lauderdale?"

He shrugs and makes his constipated De Niro face. "They offered me a good job."

Dad reaches into the back and brings Boudica onto his lap as we drive across Alligator Alley. We listen to music, and as he sings along with some of the songs, I get flashes of the Biggie I remember. I let him tell me stories I've already heard, and I don't disagree when he tells me that The Flying Burrito Brothers were the all-time greatest band.

When we reach Picayune Strand, I pay the admission fee using the provided envelopes at the ranger station. I tuck in a couple of dollars, seal the envelope, and drop it into an iron box. It's an honor system, but I've never seen anybody not pay.

Even though the weather is hot and the day is dry as a bone, the trails are mushy, and Dad grins nonstop as we slosh through puddles and spin through mud. In one spot, we roll up the windows and I drive fast through a deep spot, the water splashing over the Jeep like a car wash, and Biggie laughs his ass off.

Stella calls my phone as we sit on folding chairs in a dry clearing beside a canal, drinking water and taking in nature. Herons and cranes creep along the water's edge for fish and snails. The dry grass rustles in the breeze. Boudica stalks a tiny anole lizard.

I don't have a lot of bars, so I hope the call won't drop. "Hey there."

"What are you two doing today?"

"We're off-roading in Picayune Strand."

"What?" She sounds alarmed. "I don't know if that's a good idea, Carla. What if something goes wrong?"

"Stella, it's okay. He's having a good day."

She doesn't respond right away, and I feel like a guilty kid. "Good days can become bad days pretty darn fast. Just . . . be aware."

"I will," I say. "Do you want to talk to Biggie?"

"I sure do."

I hand the phone to Dad, who lights up at the sound of her voice. On paper, they don't make sense as a couple. She spends a lot of time on hair and clothes and makeup, while Dad's hair doesn't look like it's ever met a comb, and his idea of dressed up is a pair of clean jeans. She sings church songs when she's cooking, while he is steeped in Southern rock. But scratch the surface and you'll find the two biggest, softest, kindest hearts in the world. You'll find two people who were made for each other.

My thoughts automatically go to Eamon. Spending time with him was like someone dropped a filter in front of the world, making everything more vivid and clear. My mouth still wants to smile when I think about him. My heart still picks up speed. I know that in time it will pass—the way it did with Camilo Vega—but right now I wish Eamon was here.

"Love you, too," Dad says, before disconnecting the call and handing over the phone. He gives me a wry grin. "I don't think she's real happy with us right now."

I laugh. "Ya think?"

"We should probably head back."

"Yeah, you're right," I say, sadness washing over me. "Do you want to take Forty-One back? It's the long way, but we could grab a bite at Joanie's on the way."

"We're already in trouble, so why not?"

•　　•　　•

As I pull into the driveway, Biggie is asleep with his head tipped against the window, his mouth open, and snores rolling out like thunder. Between the off-road excitement, the long drive, and an order of frog legs at Joanie's Blue Crab Café, he's completely worn out. It may have been too much.

Despite trying to wake him gently, I startle him into consciousness and he stares at me with wild eyes until his brain has had a chance to catch up. "Jesus, you scared me."

"I'm sorry," I say. "We're home."

We've been ignoring the reminders on Biggie's watch most of the day, but now it chimes, indicating that it's time for his medications. We go in the house, and while Dad takes his pills, I feed the kitten. Cathleen told me to keep offering wet food until Boudica's eating enough that she no longer needs the bottle. I'm not sure what constitutes enough, but she seems to like nibbling bits of food off the tip of my finger.

"Thanks for today," Biggie says. "I really enjoyed it."

"Me, too."

As he envelops me in a bear hug, tears spring up in my eyes. Today was such a good day that it makes me wonder if Stella is too exhausted to see things objectively. Maybe my being here is a good thing. Maybe it will help him remember.

Chapter 19

Anna calls the following morning while I'm going through the boxes that Stella pulled out of storage, while keeping an eye on Biggie through my bedroom window.

"How are things going?" Anna asks, as I open the lid to an entire shoebox of dried Valentine's Day carnations. Some of them are from old friends, but several are from boys who are now married with kids. I don't even know who some of them are anymore.

"Great," I say, explaining that Stella went to Key West for a few days and describing my trip with Dad to Picayune Strand. "It's a little strange sleeping in my old room, and I'm trying to figure out why I kept so much sentimental crap. I mean, seriously, I have ticket stubs but no idea what movies they were from. And programs from basketball games. Why?"

"Because we humans like keeping tangible reminders of

intangible moments," Anna says. "And I think it's good to have some keepsakes, but it's important to know which of them are emotional anchors. Those you can let go."

Nearly a year after Ben's death, she carried nearly all the keepsakes from their relationship to a small beach in Trinidad and burned them. She explained to me later that she didn't need them when Ben was still alive in her heart and in her memories.

But what happens when you lose your memories?

"When are you making your crossing?" I ask, changing the subject as I carry the box of dead flowers outside to the garbage can.

"Within the next few weeks," she says. "The boat is ready, but I think Keane is a little reluctant to leave. He hasn't spent this much time with his family in years. Right now, he's down at the pub, running the bar so Ciara can have some time to herself."

"Have you considered staying?"

"No longer than a minute," Anna says. "Keane's got a job waiting for him in St. Petersburg, and I've been doing an online course in nonprofit organization management. Our future's not in Ireland."

"It'll be nice having you in the same state again."

"It's going to be strange living on dry land," she says. "But I'm looking forward to being able to see you and my mom regularly."

"Me, too," I say, before taking a deep breath and asking the question I've been avoiding. "How's, um—how's Eamon?"

"Mostly okay," Anna says, after a long pause. "He and his boss have already hammered out a remote position within the company, so he'll be able to work from the road, and he starts a ten-week car maintenance course next Thursday."

"I'm really glad he's following through."

"Keane thinks Eamon's process is a little anal retentive." Anna gives a small laugh. "But as someone who grabbed a bunch of useless shit from the grocery store and went to sea, I admire that Eamon has a plan. He's excited about traveling. He's also a little heartbroken."

"I didn't mean to hurt him."

"I know," she says. "And I think he understands, but . . ."

"Same."

"Really?"

"Between Biggie's dementia and my feelings for Eamon, I wish I could have my heart removed so it would stop aching for a little while," I say. I let out a shaky breath, realizing I've stepped way out onto an emotional ledge, but Anna responds with a sympathetic sound.

"Maybe you should tell Eamon that." Her tone is cautious, gentle.

"What's the use?" I ask. "There's no way of knowing how much time my dad has left, so I'm here indefinitely."

"Putting your travels on hold makes sense," she says. "But

I assume you're not suddenly going to be Biggie's caregiver every minute of the day when Stella has been managing it for years," she says. "Eamon could be part of your life in Florida if you let him. At least until . . ."

My nonremovable heart constricts as her words fade. Until Biggie dies. This is not something I want to think about, much less talk about. Not even with Anna.

"Look, Eamon and I weren't together long enough to even know if what we felt was real," I say in a rush. "And his plans have never included me, so there's no way in hell I'd ask him to put them aside and move to Fort fucking Lauderdale. He'll get over me. I'll get over him. Life will go on."

Anna is silent.

"I'm sorry," I say.

"No, I'm sorry for pushing," she says. "I just saw how happy the two of you seemed together and thought—"

"I know," I say, more gently this time. "I need to go now. Biggie is almost finished with his morning laps."

"Love you."

"Love you back," I say, before disconnecting and heading around back to the pool.

•   •   •

I make chocolate chip pancakes—one of Biggie's specialties—for breakfast, and after the dishes are loaded in the dishwasher, we take a drive up A1A from Seventeenth Street to the Pompano Beach Fishing Pier. I park the Jeep and we go on foot to the pier.

"Do you remember all the times you brought me here as a kid?" I ask, as we pass under the pier arch. Since the last time we were here together, the original pier was rebuilt. Decades of decay and being battered by hurricane winds finally took their toll.

"Sure," Biggie says, but I can hear the uncertainty in his tone. He wants me to think he remembers, even if he doesn't.

"We had a season pass," I remind him. "Every few months we'd pick up some bait and a couple glass bottles of Mexican Coke, and fish until we caught enough mutton snapper and bluefish for dinner. To this day, the only soda I ever drink is Mexican Coke."

"We had a lot of fun together," he says, but offers no memories to go along with mine. After yesterday, it's a little disheartening.

"Do you feel like fishing?" I ask. "Maybe they rent poles at the bait shop."

"Nah, but I wouldn't mind watching the birds."

We walk all the way out to the end of the pier and sit on a bench, watching pelicans drop like feathered bombs into the ocean and seagulls skim along the surface, snatching tiny fish. I tell Biggie the story of how a pelican once got itself tangled in his fishing line.

"He was sitting on the railing with the line wrapped

around his beak," I say. "You grabbed him before he could fly away, restrained him between your thighs, and held him still so another fisherman could cut the line."

"Was the pelican all right?"

"Oh, yeah. He ruffled his feathers a little, squawked, and flew off."

Biggie closes his eyes as he smiles, probably imagining the scene since he doesn't seem able to recall it.

I share another story about the time he took me to Lake Tahoe, where he met up with an army buddy who lived nearby. While Dad and Chuck were grilling burgers and drinking beer, I was sitting on a blanket, drying off after a swim in the lake, when a black bird came hopping toward me. I didn't know it at the time, but it was someone's pet crow, just looking for a snack. But I was only about seven years old, and this creature was coming straight at me. Not knowing how to make it go away, I opened my mouth and let out a full-throated scream, and the bird shrieked in reply. I screamed again and the crow did the same. Over and over, kid and corvid, we screamed at each other until the owner appeared and took the bird away.

Biggie laughs as hard as he did that day at Lake Tahoe. "Why didn't I help you?"

"You were probably too busy laughing your ass off," I say, smiling. "And eventually the owner realized his crow was terrorizing a small child and came for it."

"You know what you'd call that, don't you?" Biggie asks, nudging me with his elbow. I shake my head, and he grins. "A screaming bloody murder."

I groan, which makes him chuckle, and I elbow him back. "Ready to hit the road?"

Biggie nods. "Always."

We stop at the bait shop for bottles of Mexican Coke that we drink in the Jeep on the drive back to the house. Biggie heads to his room for a nap, while I go to the front porch and call my boss about a job.

"We're not busy enough right now for another bartender," Craig says, when he comes to the phone. "But if you wanted to wait tables, I could start you on the floor as soon as you want."

I really, really hate the waitress uniforms. They're uncomfortable, sexist, and just . . . tacky as fuck. But I spent part of my summer travel money on a bridesmaid's dress for Anna's wedding, along with a flight to Ireland and the hotel room. I'm not in immediate danger of going broke, but this is a good chance for me to build up a little bit of savings for once. "Okay, fine. But I can't start until the weekend."

"No problem," Craig says. "You're still in the system, so I'll get you on the schedule. You'll need to swing by at some point, though, to find just the right size uniform."

Most of the time he's a decent boss who doesn't throw fits if someone calls out sick or needs a day off after the schedule has already been made, but he's kind of obsessive when it comes to the uniforms.

"Hey, Craig . . ."

"Yeah?"

"I just threw up in my mouth a little," I say. "Also, I never brought Anna's uniforms back after she left. So, I'll just wear those."

He's spluttering in protest as I disconnect.

I text Anna.

> Who's the sexy pirate now, bitch?

> Don't let it be you. Don't let it be you. Don't let it be you. Don't let it be you.

> It's me!

> Craig is going to freak when he sees your short hair.

> I know, right? And I'm living for it.

A few minutes later, Stella calls to check up on Biggie and me. I tell her that he's napping, but I don't want to worry her, so I don't tell her about our trip to the pier. I know her schedule makes sense, but I can't help wondering if revisiting old places might help jog his memory. Buy him more time. At the very least it would be more fun than endless rewatches of *Easy Rider* and reading the same books over and over. Dad may be getting up there in age, but he's always been active, and he's not an invalid.

"How's Key West?"

"It's been such a treat." She sighs. "Sleeping alone for a change. Sleeping all night. I did some shopping on Duval Street, and I even drank a margarita last night with dinner."

I laugh. "Stella gone wild."

"Check-out is tomorrow at eleven, so I should be home by midafternoon," she says. "Unless you want me to come home sooner."

"I've needed this time with Dad as much as you needed the break," I say. "And after you get home, it's back to work for me, so don't rush."

"In that case, I'll probably stop for lunch at that place in Key Largo with the triggerfish tacos."

"Go bananas, Stell."

She giggles. "Love ya, see ya, bye."

When she's gone, I pick up my phone and pull up Eamon's Instagram account. His most recent photo is one I took of him sitting on the hood of the Land Rover the morning we were held up by the sheep. The post is an introduction, explaining that he's about to embark on a trip around the world in a 1973

Series III Defender. The photos immediately before that are all pictures of the time we spent together. Mostly nature shots and pictures of the Rover, but the very first photo on his feed is the picture of the two of us in the woods. As if his existence began at that moment. Which is silly because social media is not real life, but I can't help feeling like that moment *was* the beginning of something real.

Chapter 20

The morning Stella is due back, I come out of my room, expecting Dad to be wearing his swim trunks, ready to do his laps, but he's not in the living room. I poke my head into the bedroom, but he's not asleep, and there's no sound of the shower running in his bathroom. He's not in the kitchen. I glance out the window to see if he's already swimming without me, but he's not in the pool, either. When I notice the front door is open, my brain goes into panic mode, remembering what he said about not being able to go for walks alone because he gets lost. I shove my feet into a pair of flip-flops and rush outside. I sprint to the bottom of the driveway and scan the street, but Biggie is nowhere to be seen.

I dash back into the house long enough to grab my phone and car keys, before jumping into the Jeep. I drive slowly through the winding streets of Sailboat Bend, searching the spaces between houses in case he decided to stop and admire someone's flower bed. I don't know what he's wearing. I don't know if he has any sort of identification with him. It isn't likely that he'd wander into the middle of traffic or fall into the river, but the simple thought of him being disoriented and afraid is physically painful. It feels like my heart is in a vise and someone just keeps twisting. And it hits me suddenly, hits me hard, that sparing his child from confusion and fear was exactly why he made the choices he did. I realize, right now, that I would do anything to keep *him* from feeling lost and alone.

I've been circling the neighborhood for the better part of an hour when my phone rings with a call from Stella.

"Carla, honey," she says. "I just got a call from the police—"

"Oh God, Stella. I lost him!" I wail. "I'm so, so sorry."

"Calm down," she says, gently. "Biggie is safe. He's at the station up on Broward because he was found standing at the corner, asking people for directions to the pier."

Guilt lodges in my throat at the mention of the pier.

"They tried to take him home," Stella continues. "But you were already out looking for him."

"I must have forgotten to lock the door last night."

"Hey, don't beat yourself up. This isn't the first time this has happened," she says, which only makes me feel worse because she's been carrying this weight all by herself for years. Then I come home, all sure that I can somehow fix Biggie, and lose him after only three days. "Your dad was a little belligerent when they picked him up, so he might not recognize you when you get there. Just talk calmly and matter-of-factly, okay? I'm leaving Key West now, so I'll be there soon."

On the short drive to the police station, I realize I'm only wearing a bikini and flip-flops. I pull the Jeep to the side of the road and go around to the back. Years ago, when Biggie outfitted the cargo area for traveling, he built a low platform and installed drawers underneath. He kept cooking supplies and nonperishable foods in there, but I use the drawers as a dresser. Which is where I find an old white tank top that belongs in its own realm of wrinkled and a pair of men's plaid boxers I don't remember acquiring.

When I reach the station, I'm adequately covered in the loosest sense of the word—and I'm not sure I'd release a man suffering from dementia into my custody right now—but I forge ahead, telling the receptionist at the main desk that I'm here to pick up my wayward father.

The officer who responded to the original call comes to meet me and fills me in on the details as he leads me down a long hallway.

"He was standing on the corner of Broward and Palm, asking everyone who passed if they knew the way to the pier. He didn't specify which pier, but when I questioned him at the scene, he told me he was going fishing with Carla."

"That's me," I say. "We went to the Pompano Beach Fishing Pier yesterday, so he must have been confused."

"He got a little belligerent when I asked him to get in the squad car," the officer says. "I tried to assure him he wasn't being arrested and suggested we walk to the station, since it was down the street, but he just kept asking for a lawyer."

"That sounds like Biggie."

"It took two of us to get him in the car," the officer continues. "And he managed to fit an impressive amount of curse words in during the short time it took us to get back to the station."

"That tracks, too."

He stops in front of a metal door beside a one-way window. "He seems to have calmed down since we brought him in, but I couldn't tell you where his thoughts are right now."

Biggie is sitting at a table, wearing jeans and a T-shirt that says DON'T MAKE ME REPEAT MYSELF. —HISTORY. It's one of his favorites. They've given him a cup of coffee and a sprinkle doughnut that's mostly uneaten. He doesn't look agitated, he looks defeated.

"Are you the lawyer they assigned to me?" he asks, eyeing me skeptically.

Stella warned me that I should always assume he doesn't remember me, so I say, "No, I'm here to drive you home."

He pushes away from the table and stands. He's always been larger than life to me, but now he seems small. "I'm Douglas Black, but most people call me Biggie."

"It's nice to meet you, Biggie. I'm Carla."

"I have a daughter named Carla," he says. "When she was a little girl, I used to take her to the pier for fishing."

The one thing I didn't tell him yesterday was that I was always slightly afraid of the pier, mostly because it was so high off the water, and it seemed like a long way to fall. I always stayed close to Biggie, because I knew that as long as he was there, nothing could hurt me. He would never let me fall. "I bet that was fun."

"I can't remember how to get there."

"Were you trying to go fishing?"

His eyebrows pull together, and he frowns. "I don't . . . I don't remember."

"Well," I say, smiling at him. "It's a good thing you weren't out walking around in your tighty-whities."

He laughs. "No one needs to see that."

I sign the release papers, and we walk outside to the Jeep.

"Wow, this takes me back," Biggie says, resting his hand on the hood. "I used to have a rig just like this. I called her Valentina."

"That's a coincidence," I say, as the vise of sadness tightens around my heart again. "My Jeep is called Valentina, too. After my dad's favorite hot sauce."

He gets in the passenger seat and fastens the belt. When I start the engine, he closes his eyes to listen. I don't know what he hears, but it must be something familiar because when he looks at me, he says, "This was my Jeep, wasn't it?"

"Yes."

"Did I give it to you?"

"You did."

"You're my Carla."

I nod, unable to keep the tears from spilling over. "I'm your Carla."

He unfastens his seat belt, leans over, and hugs me hard, letting me cry on his shoulder like he's always done. At any age. For any reason.

"I'm sorry," he says, when we finally pull out of the parking lot and head toward home. "I didn't mean to cause trouble."

"You don't ever have to apologize, Biggie. None of this is your fault."

He's quiet on the drive, and I realize that there were so many questions I should have asked before I shooed Stella off to Key West. I should have paid closer attention to the instructions in her glittery folder. Was what just happened to Biggie like a drunk blackout that doesn't exist in his memories? When he apologizes, does he remember why?

"This is what I didn't want you to see," he says, as we pull into the driveway.

"If I'm ever going to be a functioning adult, I need to be able to face the hard stuff."

Biggie snorts. "I'm a fucking old man, and I still haven't mastered it, so if you crack the code, let me know."

"I would," I say, giving him a small smile. "But you'd just forget."

He barks a laugh and reaches out like he might ruffle my hair, then pulls back self-consciously, like maybe he doesn't fully trust the muscle memory. "How'd I end up with you as my kid?"

"You got lucky, I guess."

•   •   •

Dad and I are listening to Frank Turner—one of the rare contemporary songwriters we both agree is outstanding—when Stella arrives. He took a short nap after we returned home from the police station, and we've spent the past hours drinking lemonade and talking. Biggie's been telling me stories I already know by heart while I've shared stories from the road that he's probably already forgotten.

"What's this I hear about you getting hauled to the slammer?" Stella teases, as she comes in through the front door, suitcase rolling behind her. Sunshine seems to follow her, along with the eternal cloud of Charlie perfume.

Biggie brightens when he sees her. "Glad you made it home safe."

"I could say the same for you." She takes him by the chin and kisses him, but she doesn't press for details he may not be able to supply. "I missed you, Big."

"I missed you, too."

"I bet you say that to all the girls."

"Nah," he says, blushing a little. "Only you."

Despite spending the past four hours in her car, Stella insists on making lunch and gently eases Biggie back into his normal routine, never once treating him like a child or an invalid, and I realize that my assumptions about Dad's care were wrong. She tells him how she took the trolley tour of Key West and went to Mallory Square for sunset, and together they scroll through the pictures on her phone.

Later, after she's made sure he's comfortable for the night, Stella plops down on the couch beside me with two glasses of Moscato. Typically, I avoid it because it makes my teeth ache, but when she offers, I take the glass.

"I might have jumped into this caregiver thing too fast," I say.

"That's on me." She takes a big gulp of wine. "I was so emotionally exhausted that when you came home, I saw a chance to take a break and ran for the hills. I'm sorry I left you unequipped."

"I'm sorry you've had to do this by yourself for so long."

"Oh, honey." Stella rests her hand on my cheek. "I knew what I was getting into when I married him. It was right there in the wedding vows."

I lean into the touch. "Thank you."

"I saw that you updated your Instagram while I was

away," she says, changing the subject to another difficult topic. "What's his name?"

"Eamon Sullivan," I say. "Best man."

Her eyebrows arch. "And was he?"

I take a sip of wine and wince at the cloying sweetness. "Yes."

"Well, come on, spill the tea."

"*Spill the tea?*"

"That's what all the kids are saying now, right?"

I laugh. "I hate to break it to you, Stella, but you're not one of the kids. Hell, I'm not even one of the kids anymore."

She levels a look at me. "You've never posted a picture of yourself with a man on your Instagram and the comments are blowing up. You're in love and I think you want everyone to know. You're practically begging to talk about it."

"You got all of that from a few photos?" I say. "That's ridiculous."

"All I'm sayin' is that he must be something special to make you want to run *home*."

"He made me realize that I needed to stop running."

"So, where is he now?"

"He's in Ireland, where he belongs," I say. "And after he gets his shit together, he's going to get in his Land Rover and travel the world. Just like I used to."

"Past tense?"

"I've lost a lot of time with Biggie. I don't want to regret not being here when . . ." I trail off and swallow hard. "I think I need to stay here for a while."

Her smile softens and her eyes are sad as she pats my thigh. "I understand. The meds aren't keeping up like they used to. But there's no telling how fast the decline will be, so you don't have to become a hermit."

"Anna basically said the same thing," I tell her. "But I don't have the capacity for a relationship right now."

"Well, I'm going to have to call bullshit on that," Stella says. "My relationship has only one painful outcome, but I wouldn't trade my time with Biggie for anything in the world. You have options, Carla. If your relationship is challenging or messy for a time, who cares? If you love him, it will be worth it."

"It's not fair to him."

Her laugh has a bitter edge. "Oh, honey, that's just part of life. Maybe you need to let Eamon decide for himself whether this situation is unfair."

"Can we not talk about this anymore?" I fiddle with a loose thread in the sofa.

"Just like your father," she says, pinching my cheek softly. "Once the emotional rope bridge starts swaying in the breeze, you're gripping the rails, ready to turn back."

"God, you're mean," I say, laughing.

Stella scrunches up her shoulders, giving me an impish grin. "I'm just spilling the tea."

Chapter 21

"No," Craig says, when I walk through the front door of the restaurant on my first day back to work, wearing a leather bandolier strapped across my chest and a pair of black powder pistols resting at my hips. The official uniform, with its low-cut bodice and ruffled too-short skirt, is beneath it all, but my hair is spiked with pomade and my black eyeliner is so on point that Killian Jones would weep. "You absolutely cannot wear those. It's against corporate policy."

"This is not a nationwide chain, Craig," I say. "There's no employee handbook, and *corporate* is the one guy who owns this dump, and I guarantee he would love this look."

"It's not sexy. It's intimidating."

"Exactly," I say. "It sends a clear message to customers that if they touch me, I will shoot them."

His eyes widen with alarm. "Those things aren't loaded, are they?"

"Do you really think I would bring loaded firearms to work?"

"I'm sorry, but I can't allow this," Craig says.

"Okay, so put me behind the bar and we'll forget this ever happened."

"I really don't have the payroll for that, so . . . fine." He shakes his head, laughing a little. "You can keep the guns, as long as they don't leave the belt . . . thing."

"Bandolier," I correct. "By the way, there are no breasts in the world big enough to make the food here taste good."

"The uniforms are meant to distract customers from how they could have eaten somewhere better."

I tilt my head. "Why don't you just fix the food?"

"Because customers don't come here for the quality," Craig says. "They come here for the tits."

"I hate this place."

"And yet you keep coming back every season."

"The tips are great."

Craig shrugs. "Tits."

Later, during my dinner break, I'm seated on an overturned milk crate beside the kitchen door when one of the line cooks, Miguel, comes outside with a plastic storage container of food. "I heard you were coming back to work, so I brought these for you."

I pull back the lid with anticipation. Every Saturday, his wife, Mercedes, makes tamales for the family to eat after church on Sunday, and every Saturday night that Miguel and I work together, he brings me a serving. I inhale deeply and sigh.

"You are a god," I say, unwrapping the corn husk from the tamale on top.

He hands me a fork. "My wife is the god."

"I still think the two of you should open your own restaurant."

"There are already so many taquerias," he says, shaking his head. "And Merce's tamales are only for her family."

"We've never met in person, so why would she consider me family?"

Miguel turns over a second milk crate and sits. Back when we both smoked, we'd take smoke breaks and talk about Mexico. Now, he says, "There isn't just one kind of family, you know? There's the people you find along the way. I've told her all about you, and she appreciates the way you respect our culture and our country. You're not just some white girl taking selfies in Tulum."

I laugh at that but feel a catch in my chest at the thought of being someone's found family. And at how much bigger my own found family might be if I hadn't been so afraid of losing people. "I'm honored. Thank you."

"Also, Merce thinks you need to do something else with your life."

I snort a laugh. "Like what? I'm not exactly qualified for an actual career. I mean, I could probably deliver pizza or be a rideshare driver, but wait . . . no . . . the Jeep's too old for that."

"There must be something in that big brain that you want," Miguel says. "All I know is that you're too smart for this place."

"I could work the pole at Vixen's Cabaret. Fully nude until six A.M."

He laughs. "Do you know how to work a pole?"

"Sadly, no," I say. "So, I guess I'm going to have to marry the owner of this dump and kill him off after he puts me in the will. Then I'll fire Craig, put you in charge, buy a caftan, and spend my days seducing younger men on Miami Beach."

"That's quite a vivid fantasy," a voice behind us says through the screen door. Craig. "But Amber is about to seat a table in your section, so you'll have to save it for another day."

Leaving Miguel, I go back into the restaurant, but as I continue my shift, my thoughts keep drifting back to our conversation. I always believed working here was my career. Anna and I bonded over the fact that this place wasn't a stepping-stone to something bigger and better. Seasonal bartending has made my travels possible. But now Anna is preparing to build a nonprofit organization with her husband, and as I stand at

table eleven wearing a sexy pirate costume, my future suddenly seems . . . pathetic.

●　　●　　●

Although I didn't get home from work until nearly midnight,
in the morning I get up with Biggie to do laps in the pool. It's
become a routine, and even though we're too busy swimming
to talk, just being together is nice.

While Dad and Stella are doing some yard work, I browse
a few job websites. Tutors and delivery drivers are in high demand, and there are plenty of positions in the medical field
that I'm not qualified for, but there is nothing in between
that speaks to me. And when I think about my interests, I'm
not sure there's an income-generating space for a beer-drinking
surf nomad who lives in her car most of the year.

"You'll figure it out," Stella says, when they come inside
and find me with my forehead resting against my desk. "You're
still young."

"I'm not sure thirty-three counts as young anymore."

"It does when you're . . ." Dad trails off and chuckles.
"However old I am."

"You're seventy-three, Big."

"All I'm saying is that you've got time," Stella continues,
but while they head to the kitchen for lunch, I call Anna.

"If I wasn't a bartender, what would I be?" I ask.

"Oh, wow. I was not expecting that question," she says, then pauses to consider. "I could imagine you doing something outdoors-related. Maybe working at a camping outfitter or even as a park ranger, but I could also see you teaching English abroad. They're always looking for teachers in Japan and Korea. That would be a way to travel and make money at the same time."

"How is it that everyone knows me better than I know myself?"

"It's ridiculously easy to get in your own way," Anna says. "Ask me how I know."

I laugh. "Good point."

"Thinking about making a career change?"

"Do you remember Miguel, the line cook at the restaurant?"

"Yes."

"His wife says I need to find something else to do with my life," I say. "But what if I'm too old for that? What if I end up being the oldest bartender in Fort Lauderdale? I used to think I didn't care, but . . . I don't want that."

Anna is quiet for a beat.

"There's only one day in your life when it will be too late for you to make a change," she says, a note of sadness in her voice. "Ask me how I know *that*."

"I know."

"You may still end up being the oldest person doing something, but it should be something you love."

"Thank you."

"Always."

The call ends and I return to the internet, this time with a more focused search. As I scroll through descriptions of online courses, with Boudi curled up in my lap, I think about Eamon, currently disentangling himself from his normal life so he can go explore the world, while I'm doing the exact opposite. Being those proverbial ships that pass in the night is a bittersweet feeling, and I miss him. I think about calling. I even pick up my phone. But as it prompts me to enter my passcode, I wonder if talking to him would be like rubbing salt in my own wound.

Later, when I have something that resembles a plan, I find Biggie and Stella watching court shows in the living room. Stella is basically addicted to reality TV drama. She mutes the television at the commercial break.

"I've been doing some research," I tell them. "And I found a program where I can take the prerequisites and general coursework online, then transfer to campus-based learning for the core curriculum and fieldwork."

"What are you considering?" Stella asks.

"Forestry, with an eye toward being a ranger or maybe even fire service," I say, looking to my dad for . . . approval, a reaction, *anything* to let me know he remembers what a huge role he's played in my life. I wouldn't even be considering this if he hadn't shown me that world.

Biggie beams at me, his eyes shiny as he nods.

"I'm still in the planning stages, but—"

"We'll need to go shopping for school supplies," Stella says, rubbing her hands together, and I can picture her barreling through Target, snapping up a rainbow of gel pens and notebooks with unicorns on the cover.

"Slow your roll, Lisa Frank," I say. "I need to apply and be admitted after being out of high school for fifteen years and working in a completely unrelated field. And if I manage to jump those hurdles, I still need to find a way to pay for everything."

Biggie clears his throat. "I, um—I've been putting money aside. Just in case."

"Are you telling me I have a college fund?"

"It's not a lot," Stella says. "But it's enough to get you started."

"Okay . . . so . . . I'm going to college then." My heart swells at the thought.

"This calls for some bubbly!" Stella hustles to the kitchen, leaving Biggie and me alone.

"You are smart, independent, and cool as all hell, despite my fucked-up efforts at raising you," he says, dabbing at his eyes with the old red bandanna he keeps in the pocket of his jeans. "There has never been a time when I haven't been proud of you, but watching you figure your shit out . . . I've never been prouder."

In the kitchen I can hear the cork pop on a bottle of sparkling cider—because no more alcohol for Biggie Black—and glasses tinkling as Stella brings them down from the cupboard. All the while, the tears are coming too fast for me to keep up.

"Thank you," I say. "I love you, Biggie. If you remember nothing else, remember that."

He puts his big hand to his big chest, big fingers splayed over his even bigger heart. "Even when you're gone from my mind, you will always be here."

Chapter 22

I'm awake before my alarm when I hear a soft tap on my bedroom door. At first, I think it's Biggie, coming to fetch me for our morning swim, but Stella's voice comes through the door, soft and muffled. "Carla, honey."

Her morning-person cheerfulness is conspicuously absent, and I wonder if Biggie is already having a rough day. It hasn't happened to me yet, but Stella says that sometimes he flat-out refuses to get out of bed.

I open my bedroom door to find her standing in the hallway. She's still wearing her pink polka-dot pajamas, and the quilted sleep mask with her name embroidered across the front has slipped down around her neck. She's not wearing any makeup, and tears are streaming down her cheeks.

"What's wrong?" I ask, worried that Biggie got violent

and accidentally hurt her, but she has no visible redness or bruising.

"Biggie's gone."

I glance down at the tank top and boy shorts I wore to bed. "Let me put on some clothes and find my keys. Do you know how long—"

"No, sweetheart." She takes a deep breath and her voice shakes as she says, "He died during the night."

I sit down hard on the edge of the bed. "That—that can't be right."

Boudica pounces into my lap and Stella's eyes look endlessly sad. "He didn't wake up."

"But we were going fishing today," I say. "I bought the licenses and poles."

Even though I know Stella isn't lying to me, the idea that Biggie would be dead doesn't make sense. He was alive yesterday. He was fine.

"I've already called for an ambulance." She sits beside me.

"You must be mistaken."

"Oh, honey, I'd wish on every star in the sky to be wrong about this."

"Are you sure? Maybe—"

"Carla." She puts her hand on my thigh to keep me from going to check. "He's gone."

I fall back on the bed, still holding Boudi. "Fucking Biggie."

Stella twists her torso to look at me. "What?"

"Weren't we just talking about how it was going to get harder?" I say. "Leave it to Biggie to spare us the hard days and the pain of watching him deteriorate."

"He couldn't have planned this," she says. "He probably had a stroke."

"Oh, I know. All I'm saying is that if Biggie Black had a choice in how to go out, this is what he'd choose."

Stella issues a tiny giggle, followed by a wet sniffle. "God, you're right."

"What do we do now?"

"Well, I'm probably going to cry for a good long while and put on some clothes, so the paramedics don't see me in my nightie," she says. "And then . . . I don't know. I had Biggie's life all mapped out, but I never really thought about what mine would look like after he was gone."

"Did he have a will?"

She nods. "All his paperwork is in the file cabinet, but that can wait for another day."

"Can I see him?"

"Oh, Carla, of course."

When I was a little girl, I would rise with the sun and scamper to Biggie's room to wake him, bouncing onto the end of his bed. He kept a copy of *Stardust* in the side table drawer and sometimes he'd read a few pages aloud before school. Or, if it was a weekend, I'd snuggle up with the National Parks Passport and we'd talk about which parks we planned to visit next.

Today, I walk slowly from my room to his, dreading the steps, wishing I could rewind time. But the tricky part of time travel is that there's no perfect place to stop. To save him from getting dementia, I would have to erase all the good things that have happened since. I could avoid my reckless years and stay with Biggie, but then I'd lose my travels.

I'd lose Eamon Sullivan.

I crack open the door, half-hoping Biggie will be sitting up in bed, his glasses perched on the tip of his nose, reading Doris Kearns Goodwin. Instead, his body is still, and his confused brain is at rest. He looks like he's at peace.

Tears gather, then fall, and I sit on the edge of the bed, trying to imagine life without Biggie, but all I can see is the giant empty space he once filled. His hand holds a lingering warmth, like there might be the tiniest bit of him still left inside his body, so I give it a gentle squeeze.

The paramedics arrive and I move out of their way. They verify that he is dead. They carry him off. I move around the house for the next several hours in a fog of disbelief, with Stella on the periphery of my awareness, making the arrangements for his cremation. I turn on the stereo, but without Biggie, the music sounds distorted. I turn it off and go to my room, where I cry until I'm empty. Until I fall asleep.

The next time I wake, Stella is sitting on the couch, eating from a plate of lasagna. She's dressed, but I've never seen her go a whole day without makeup or eat somewhere other than the dining room table with a napkin on her lap.

"How are you feeling?" I ask, sitting beside her.

"I've always known this day was coming," she says. "I didn't think it would happen this soon, but I've had time to mentally prepare. So, I'm . . . heartbroken, but surviving. How 'bout you?"

"The day I came home, Biggie mistook me for my mom," I tell her. "He spoke some hard truths about himself and her . . . and me . . . but I guess you could call it closure. I'm grateful for that, even if I'm pissed that he's gone."

"Pissed is valid. Feel all the feelings, Carla. Let them hurt, then let them heal."

"You're very wise," I say. "Like if Yoda and Dolly Parton had a baby."

"That would be one weird baby."

"Exactly."

Stella laughs so hard that we both end up crying again, but this time there's a little bit of hope mixed into the sadness.

• • •

It's the middle of the night in Ireland when I call Anna, but she answers.

"I'm sorry to wake you," I say. "But . . . Biggie died."

"What?" She sounds confused at first, until my words click into place. "Oh God, no. Carla, I'm so, so sorry. What happened?"

"He had a massive stroke in his sleep."

"How are you holding up?"

"I haven't even been home that long," I say. "If I had come back sooner—"

"Don't go down that road," Anna warns, and I hear the steel inside the softness. "There's no 'if only' that will bring him back, and letting yourself get caught up in that kind of thinking isn't healthy. You made a lifetime of happy memories with your dad. Remember those instead."

"If there's any consolation, it's that he died still remembering me."

She sniffles and her voice breaks when she says, "That's the one. Hold on to that forever."

"He always—" I say, then stop, reminding myself of the time difference. "I should let you get back to sleep."

"It's okay," Anna says. "I never get tired of hearing Biggie stories."

She lets me talk for a long time, until I'm exhausted enough to sleep, which is probably sunrise in her part of the world. "I'm sorry I kept you up all night."

"Hush," she says. "Consider it his eulogy."

"I really don't deserve you," I say, before I can start crying again. "I'm going to let you go now."

"Love you."

"Love you back."

•　　•　　•

Despite her ditzy appearance and her glittery folders, Stella is a highly organized person. In a matter of days, the very few salvageable items from his wardrobe have been donated to Goodwill, and she adds a box of his old band T-shirts to the growing stack in my room that still needs to be sorted.

"I thought about leaving his stuff in the closet until I felt ready to let go," she says. "But I'm not sure if that'll ever happen. I'll love Biggie until my dying day."

"I understand," I say. "His turntable and record collection are the only things I want to keep. Everything else . . . you can decide what's best."

"He left the house to you," Stella says. "You could kick me out if you wanted."

"I would never do that."

"You don't mind living here with an old lady who's not your kin? What if you want to get married and have kids in this house? I do Zumba. I might be around awhile yet."

My laughter fades to a smile as I think about what Miguel said about the family we find along the way. "You're not going anywhere, Stella. You are my kin where it counts."

Chapter 23

Biggie did not want a funeral; he wanted a party. Even before the dementia set in, when I was still a child, he'd tell me to skip the mourning, throw a kegger, and scatter his ashes in the place where I had felt closest to him.

"No soppy eulogies. No tears," he said. "I want people to remember their best times, their happiest moments with me."

Stella hires a local barbecue restaurant to serve ribs slathered in sauce, Southern-style potato salad, collard greens, mac and cheese, and key lime pie. A party supply company sets up tables around the front yard, along with a tent for the food. I order a keg of Shiner Bock—Biggie's favorite beer—and create a playlist called *Save Your Tears for Some Other Guy*.

The day of the party, I choose my dad's Flying Burrito Brothers T-shirt. It's so big I wear it like a dress, over leggings with a leather belt around my waist, but it feels like the right choice. He'd probably laugh and tell me to keep it, even though it was his favorite of all his T-shirts. He used to joke that I should save some of his ashes and sprinkle them beside Gram Parsons out in Joshua Tree. I feel a catch in my chest and tears sting my eyes, but I breathe through it.

Save your tears for some other guy, I remind myself.

"Don't you just look adorable," Stella says, as I come out of my bedroom. "Like a classic rock pixie."

I laugh. "That's not quite the vibe I was going for, but I think Biggie would approve."

Stella links her arm through mine. "He certainly would."

We go outside, where the catering team is filling the food tables with chafing dishes. It doesn't look like a funeral until I put his box of ashes on a table covered with butcher paper, where everyone is encouraged to write a farewell, song lyrics, or a favorite memory of my dad.

I write the first note: *It was always a good time, but I wish it had been a longer time.*

People come out of the woodwork to say goodbye to Biggie Black. Old army friends. Former students and colleagues. Neighbors. Ugly Louie. So many futures shaped by his wisdom. So many lives touched by his existence.

An older woman with short silver hair and oversized glasses approaches me at the keg as I'm filling a plastic party cup with Shiner.

"Are you Carla?" She cocks her head, studying my face,

and I'm seized by the sudden fear that she is my mother. She looks nothing like me, but I'm not sure I'd recognize Sheryl if she were standing in front of me at my father's wake.

"Um . . . yeah?"

"My name's Reba Ann Perry," she says. "Your dad was my older brother."

"Oh, wow." Her actual identity comes as an even bigger surprise. "Biggie didn't talk much about his family, so I never expected anyone to come."

"There was a lot of bad blood between him and our daddy, and I was young when Doug got sent to Vietnam," Reba Ann says. "But I thought the world of him as a girl, and it looks like he stayed true to the good man I remember him to be."

I nod. "He did."

"There were times I thought about reaching out, but it felt like maybe too much water had passed under the bridge. I wasn't sure if he'd want to hear from me."

"He would have loved it," I tell her. "His heart was as big as the rest of him."

Her eyes are shining behind her glasses. "Would it be okay if I gave you a hug?"

"Sure."

Reba Ann wraps her arms around me and pats me softly on the back, and just like that, my family gets a little bigger. "I'm real sorry for your loss."

"I'm sorry for your loss, too."

She steps back and squeezes my forearms as she smiles. "You don't look a bit like him."

"He used to say it was lucky I inherited his brains instead of his looks," I say, making her giggle. "I'm glad you came. Maybe someday we can meet up and fill in the blanks of my dad's life."

"I'd like that." Reba Ann pulls a tissue from the pocket of her slacks and dabs her eyes. "I know he said no crying, but I'm so happy to meet Doug's daughter."

"Happy tears don't count," I say, as Anna and Keane come into the yard through the front gate.

I didn't expect them to be here, but their presence isn't a surprise. Of course Anna would come. I just hope I haven't thrown them off schedule for their sail back from Ireland.

"I better let you go," Reba Ann says.

"Thank you." I give her another brief hug. "Take care."

I practically run across the yard, straight into Anna's embrace. "God, I'm so glad to see you."

"Are you okay?" Her voice is laced with concern.

"As fine as I can be," I say, moving from Anna to Keane, who literally lifts me off my feet. "I just don't want to drink alone."

He laughs as he digs into the pocket of his dress pants and gives Anna the car keys. He rubs his hands together. "What are we drinking?"

"I've got Shiner on tap," I tell him, as we head for the

keg. Around us, people are eating barbecue with their fingers and strangers are getting to know each other as Gram Parsons sings in the background. Biggie would be so pleased.

Anna extends a brown paper gift bag. "That reminds me. We brought a bottle of Jameson for the after-party."

"You are the wind beneath my wings."

She laughs. "Do you want me to run it inside?"

"I've got it," I say. "Grab a beer, eat some food. I'll be right back."

Leaving Anna and Keane at the keg, I continue to the house and into the kitchen, where I stash the bottle in the cupboard over the fridge.

"Got any sangria?" a male voice says.

I go still.

I turn my head to find Eamon leaning against the kitchen doorframe, looking as unbearably handsome as the first time I saw him. He might even be wearing the same olive-green button-up he wore the day we met. His presence raises so many questions that I don't even know which one to ask first. Until I realize that none of the answers matter. Eamon Sullivan crossed an ocean for me. And I'm so damn done with running away. "Oh, fuck it."

I cross the room in three steps, catch him by the front of his shirt, and pull him toward me. Unlike our first kiss at The Confession Box, there is no confusion as Eamon takes my face in his hands. His mouth is on mine as I push him backward into the living room, where we collide with the back of the couch, before stumbling to my bedroom door.

"What are you doing here?" I ask, breathless between kisses.

His back is against the door as he pauses, his hands on my hips. "Did you think I wouldn't come?"

"I thought we were finished."

The corners of his mouth turn up in the barest hint of a smile. He reaches behind him, his gaze holding mine, and opens the bedroom door. "We will never be finished."

• • •

The party is still in full swing when Eamon and I rejoin everyone in the yard, and Anna is smiling like butter wouldn't melt in her mouth, obviously in on the scheme for him to be here. He holds my hand like he has no plan to let go, and I don't mind at all. There's a tiny voice in the back of my head that says maybe it's too soon after losing my dad to be this happy. But there's a deeper, gruffer voice—it sounds a lot like Biggie—that says now is the perfect time to be happy. That every moment is the perfect time to be happy.

We eat, drink, dance, laugh, and I share every memory of my father that comes to mind, and my friends listen to stories they've heard before because they love me. The guests slowly trickle away, stopping at my table to say goodbye and offer one last sympathy.

"We should go, too," Anna says. "We're going to see Mom tomorrow, and the day after it's back to Ireland so we can sail home."

"Thank you for coming all this way for me."

"This was mighty *craic*," Keane says. "Biggie would be proud."

They leave, but Eamon stays behind, helping Stella and me refrigerate the leftovers, as the caterers pack up their chafing dishes and the party supply staff folds up the chairs. Once Stella's gone to bed, Eamon scoops up Boudica and we sit on the swing under the gumbo limbo tree.

"I've been thinking," I say. "I know you have plans, and I have some plans now, too, but Biggie always wanted me to scatter his ashes in the place I felt closest to him."

"De Soto National Forest?" Eamon says, and the world goes blurry as I realize he remembers. I lean over and kiss his cheek.

"I thought maybe you could come with me. To De Soto. To Joshua Tree to see the stars. And to Tierra del Fuego."

Eamon pulls back and looks at me, realizing that what I'm asking is for him to put his Land Rover plans on hold and travel with me in the Jeep. A slow smile spreads across his face, making his cheek dimple.

"I'll go anywhere in the world," he says. "As long as it's with you."

Chapter 24

Eamon Sullivan and I stand on a rocky beach at Estancia Moat, where there is nothing but a lonely Argentine Coast Guard outpost and the ocean. Boudica is perched on Eamon's shoulder, wearing a sweater that Stella knitted so Boudi wouldn't get cold. In the distance, too far for us to see, is Cabo de Hornos—Cape Horn—where the Atlantic and Pacific meet. We have reached the end of the road.

The end of the world.

It's taken us nearly a year to get here, but when have we ever been known to take the direct route?

Our first major stop was De Soto National Forest, where we set up camp at the coordinates written in the margin of my National Parks Passport. We took a photo sitting together on the hood of the Jeep. We found the swimming hole and the rope swing. That evening, as the sun was setting, I poured some of Biggie's ashes on a leaf and let it drift downstream. I don't suppose he got very far before the leaf tipped over or the ashes were carried off on the breeze, but it was nice to give him one last little trip.

Back at our campsite, Eamon and I toasted the memory of Douglas John "Biggie" Black with cups of cold sangria and celebrated his life by dancing to King Harvest in the moonlight.

We camped our way across the southern United States, stopping to explore New Orleans, San Antonio, Las Cruces, and Phoenix before arriving at Joshua Tree National Park in California.

One of the reasons Biggie loved Joshua Tree was because it was the setting to a wild story in which Gram Parsons—his favorite singer and member of The Flying Burrito Brothers—had made a pact with his manager that if either of them died prematurely, the other would take the dead body to Joshua Tree and cremate it. When Gram Parsons died in 1973 from a drug overdose in a motel not far from Joshua Tree, his manager ended up stealing his corpse from LAX and driving it out to the desert before dousing it with gasoline and setting it on fire. Even though Gram Parsons is buried in Louisiana, his fans—Biggie included—still make the trek into the wilderness to leave trinkets in his memory.

Eamon and I didn't leave trinkets. I always try to follow the "leave nothing but footprints" rule when I'm out in nature.

But we did scatter some more of Biggie's ashes, and I like to think his spirit is out there somewhere, having a drink with Gram Parsons.

After Joshua Tree, we crossed the border and spent two solid months in Mexico. We went surfing in Barra de la Cruz. Got binary star tattoos in Mexico City, because maybe Anna and Keane aren't the only ones. And drank a helluva lot of tequila in the town of the same name.

We visited all the countries in Central America until we reached Panama, where we arranged to have the Jeep shipped to Turbo, Colombia. From there we followed the Pan-American Highway along the Pacific coast, through Colombia, Ecuador, Peru, Chile, and Argentina, until we finally made it to Patagonia.

We've hiked, camped, fished, and followed dozens of off-road trails, but we've also learned to balance travel and work. Eamon stops where the Wi-Fi is strong for video conferences with his team back in Ireland. And between Fort Lauderdale and Tierra del Fuego, I've learned how to do calculus, read all of Flannery O'Connor's work, and used real-world practice to earn a perfect grade in Spanish. Boudica has her own cat hammock in the Jeep, where she hangs out while we're driving.

There's a quote attributed to Mark Twain that goes, *I have found out that there ain't no surer way to find out whether you like people or hate them than to travel with them.* Eamon and I have found that we like each other very much. Sometimes we argue, but our anger is never hot enough to call it quits, never hot enough that we don't apologize.

We've spent the past four days camping just outside Ushuaia, a seaside resort town surrounded by snowcapped mountains where visitors can find boats and ships to take them on around Cape Horn, over to the Falklands, to visit an island inhabited by penguins, to see the glaciers, and even across the Drake Passage to Antarctica. Even though it's summer in the southern hemisphere, the temperature hasn't quite hit sixty degrees during the day, and the nights are blustery and cold, but we've loved every minute.

We have the remainder of Biggie's ashes with us here on this beach. He's never been to this part of the world, but his request was that I scatter the ashes wherever I felt closest to him. If not for Biggie Black, I wouldn't be standing here, at the end of the world.

Down the beach, a few penguins watch us curiously as we approach the water's edge, and Boudi's tail twitches as she watches the penguins.

"You know, a Shiner bottle probably would have been a more appropriate receptacle for Biggie's ashes," I say, making Eamon laugh. "I'm still sorry you didn't get to meet him."

"You talk about him with such affection that I can imagine him without a photo now. I'd say I've met him."

"I'm sorrier that he never met you." I extend the wooden box carved with ornate flowers. "Will you do it?"

He takes the box, rubs his thumb across the top, and looks up. The earnestness in his eyes just about kills me, and it's only one of the things I love about him. "Are you sure?"

"It seems fitting." I shrug. "He was my past. You're my foreseeable future."

"Foreseeable?" Eamon snorts a laugh. "When I told you we would never be finished, I meant it. We don't have to get married, or even live on the same continent, but you, Carla Black, are my person."

"Just scatter the ashes," I say, as I wipe my eyes on the sleeve of my sweater. Being Eamon's person is the frosting on the delicious cake of my life.

He kisses my forehead, then squats down on the beach to open the box. The wind is light and the waves licking at the tips of his boots are small as he unfolds the plastic bag of Biggie's ashes and pours the final portion into his palm. Eamon's mouth moves in a silent prayer before he lowers his hand until it's mere inches from the surface of the ocean. He opens his palm. The ashes drop into the water, sinking, mixing with the sand and stone. Becoming one with the earth again.

"He'd love the idea of being returned to the sea," I say. "He was an evolutionist who also kind of believed in reincarnation, so who knows? Maybe he'll become something that will emerge from the primordial ooze and evolve into Biggie Black again. Maybe that means there will be another me someday."

"If that happens, I hope there is also another me."

"Me, too," I say, kissing his nose. "Because you are *my* person."

Eamon gazes into the distance, in the direction of Antarctica. There are small cruise ships that make excursions during the penguin hatching and whale migration seasons. Passengers can go ashore, plant their boots on the seventh continent. Right now, we're on the cusp of the two seasons and the weather has been beautiful.

"I've been thinking," he says. "I know we're meeting Anna and Keane in Buenos Aires in two weeks, but there's a whole other continent *right there,* and when will we ever be this close to it?"

"Are you saying you want to make a detour?"

"It's only thirty-five hours to Buenos Aires," he reasons. "If we leave for Antarctica today, we'll be back in plenty of time to meet them at the airport."

"Sure." A smile spreads across my face, because I'll go anywhere in the world, as long as it's with Eamon Sullivan. "After all, what could possibly go wrong?"

Acknowledgments

Although I own my own borderline vintage Jeep Wrangler, it was my son's overland adventures in his Jeep that inspired Carla's travels, so thank you, Scott, for answering all my questions and living a life worth adapting for fiction. I promise you still have plenty of material for your own book one day.

I mentioned her in the dedication, but I owe a big thanks to the real Carla Black for letting me use her name in *Float Plan*. I had no idea she'd eventually become a main character, so I hope that fictional Carla meets with your approval.

My writing schedule was completely upended in 2021 by the arrival of a big, goofy, adorable foxhound named Harvey that I fostered from February until October, when he was finally adopted. He took up most of my mental and emotional energy, so I owe a huge thank-you to my editor, Vicki Lame, for her patience and for helping me get the book across the finish line. I couldn't have done it without you, but I wouldn't have wanted to do it without you.

St. Martin's Griffin has been an incredible home for this series, and I have so much appreciation for the team, including Vanessa Aguirre, Olga Grlic, Soleil Paz, Omar Chapa, Hannah Jones, Ginny Perrin, Diane Dilluvio, Marissa Sangiacomo, Brant Janeway, Meghan Harrington, Katy Robitzki, and Drew Kilman. Thank you, all!

Kate Schafer Testerman has been in my corner for fifteen years and she's still my dream agent. As Ted Lasso would say: I appreciate you.

I've mentioned Suzanne Young and Cristin Bishara in so many books for being the best critique partners I could have that I feel like I've run out of creative ways to say thank you. You really are the best.

Thank you to anyone who read an early draft or sent me a song that reminded you of the book or cheered me on along the way, from *Float Plan* to now. If you think this means you, it does.

My mom is one of my earliest readers and biggest supporters, and that's only one of the reasons I love her. My only regret is that now she knows I've had sex. Sorry, Mom!

Thanks to Caroline for my neglectful meal prep habits while I'm writing.

ACKNOWLEDGMENTS

Thanks to Jack for understanding that I'm not ignoring you, I'm writing.

Thanks to Talaria and Noha for being cute.

And, as always, thank you, Phil. You are my person.

About the Author

Jesi Cason Photography

Trish Doller is a writer, traveler, and dog rescuer, but not necessarily in that order. She is the international bestselling author of *Float Plan, The Suite Spot,* and *Off the Map*. She has also written several YA novels, including the critically acclaimed *Something Like Normal*. When she's not writing, Trish loves sailing, camping, and avoiding housework. She lives in southwest Florida with an opinionated herding dog and an ex-pirate. Find Trish on Twitter and Instagram @trishdoller.